antagonist, the path back home But sport is a bit different, the losses are inevitable, even for the good. And they happen a lot. Sport is central to modern culture, and these Sporting Tales are a fine, wise and fabulous insight into how sport can change the world, and how it too mirrors those very economic and social structures in their best and worst ways."

Jules Pretty, Professor of Environment and Society at the University of Essex and author of The Low-Carbon Good Life

"Sport has many stories to tell; good and bad. Sporting Tales is a stadium full of better stories about surviving and thriving in a troubled world."

Melissa Wilson, Team GB rower and co-founder of Athletes for the World

Sporting tales for troubled times...

This book is part of an on-going project initiated by the New Weather Institute to find more imaginative ways to engage with the unprecedented challenges of our times.

After decades of campaigning for a better world, the current moment seems more precarious than ever, standing on the edge of potentially irreversible ecological decline and in the grip of toxic social divisions. Athletes engaged in outdoor physical exertion find themselves particularly exposed, with their health and lives under threat from the climate extremes of a heating planet as well as the air pollution from the burning of fossil fuels responsible for climate breakdown. But sport also has an extraordinary ability and opportunity to mobilise its mass audience and appeal for change.

Sporting Tales is the fifth volume of essays and stories, following: There was a *Knock at the Door*, *Knock Twice*, *Knock Three Times*, and *Contagious Tales*. It brings together a wide variety of authors, from elite athletes to academic experts, poets, artists and activists. The collection includes contributions from several members of the Cool Down – sport for climate action network, initiated by the New Weather Institute with the Rapid Transition Alliance and supported by the KR Foundation.

Special thanks are due to John Jackson of The Argument by Design, and Nicky Saunter for production of the book, to David Boyle of The Real Press, to all the contributors, the members of Cool Down – the sport for climate action network, the Badvertising campaign, colleagues in the New Weather Institute and New Weather Sweden.

SPORTING TALES

21 new stories for a troubled world

Edited by Andrew Simms

Published in 2024 by the Real Press with the New
Weather Institute.

therealpress.co.uk

ISBN (print) 978-1-917339-00-1

ISBN (ebook) 978-1-917339-01-8

Contents

Introduction
Sport – the story maker

Andrew Simms

Sport is a story machine. Struggle. Defeat. The fall from grace. Comeback. Last minute victory. Redemption... All these vye in every unpredictable variation. As seasons, years and careers roll-by, sport constantly resets. With every refresh a new story cycle begins. Fans and players alike hunger after the new narratives endlessly offered up.

We devour rivalries, the twists of an athlete's career, the troubled relationships between managers, coaches, players, teams, supporters and even the reporters who feed us the stories, and we feed on them. Already filling to overflow every media platform from broadcast to online, newspaper and magazine stand, the more tales that are told of sport, the hungrier the audience appears to become.

Why? Sporting drama is not a niche of human experience, but a stage where, time-bound, all life is played out (typically according to arbitrary rules and conventions of our own, mostly recent, devising).

It is a kind of ritualistic theatre where the script is rewritten as the play commences, and the ending is, generally speaking, unknown, but happens within reassuringly familiar boundaries. It creates an ultimately safe, addictive form of jeopardy.

This collection celebrates the great melee of sport, the writing styles included, from poetry to essay and short story, reflects its variety. But, of course, it cannot hope, nor does it try, to be remotely comprehensive. On the contrary, a specific theme runs through these contributions, even if it is expressed in many different ways.

Pitches flooded, heat-struck players fearing for their lives, races and games rearranged to avoid the new extremes of climate, and air full of the pollution from burning fossil fuels and forests turned to tinder: sport is on the frontline of global heating.

With so many games and competitions played in the open air, both air pollution from burning fossil fuels, estimated to kill somewhere between five and over eight million people annually, and the extreme weather it worsens due to climate breakdown, now threaten athletes, fans and events alike. Reflections on this perilous condition and calls to action fill these pages on the challenges sport now grapples with. They embrace the dangers faced by athletes and sports, but also the opportunities and their responsibilities to halt the slow motion climate catastrophe.

There's something about people involved in sport that gives them a unique advantage over others when it comes to doing difficult or seemingly impossible things. Statistically, the odds in competitive sport are always stacked horribly against you – typically, there can only be one winner. But that doesn't stop millions trying. Fans too are often used to living in hope, however forlorn, for their team or favourite athlete to win, sometimes for years or a lifetime, but it doesn't stop them. There is always too, a kind of 'go for it' mentality that celebrates simply trying. Companies have been quick to exploit that sense, aligning themselves with its indomitable spirit to sell more stuff with feel-good slogans like 'just do it', and 'impossible is nothing' (it's not, of course – according to the laws of thermodynamics impossible is very much something).

And, indeed, some of the brightest glimmers of hope in recent years scarred by upheaval, war, pandemic, and division have come from sport.

Taking the knee, wearing the rainbow and calling out child food poverty are all ways in which sport has driven awareness of prejudice and injustice, and pushed social progress.

But the opposite is also true. At the elite level especially, sport has allowed itself to be a billboard for corrosive commerce, promoting everything from junk food to gambling. Violent regimes with appalling human rights records are allowed, brazenly, to use teams and events that command some of the biggest media audiences in the world to 'sportswash' their reputations. Top level sport itself has become the favoured public relations cloak of those who have the most to hide.

You can argue that this isn't new. It's true, tobacco companies were once one of sport's most prominent sponsors. But the glaring contradiction of healthy sporting activity being sponsored by an addictive product that kills led to widespread bans. So, much like a team changing tactics to overcome an obstacle or an opposition, we know that sport can adapt when it needs to. Is it asking too much?

Change – rapid transition – has never been more needed than now, with the frighteningly real prospect of losing, irretrievably, the climate that sport and all of us depend on.

Many things need to happen simultaneously. But one easy win would be for sport to stop being a billboard for the very climate polluters who are wrecking both the conditions it needs to survive, and the health of its athletes.

Yet, it seems that in every direction, in almost every stadium, or on almost every team shirt there is a fossil fuel company, car maker or airline promoting highly polluting products and lifestyles – normalising behaviour that is pushing us over a climate cliff. The good news is that voices are beginning to be raised against the practice. Campaigners globally are calling on sport to drop dirty sponsors, from African civil society working for oil company Total to be dropped as sponsor of the Africa Cup of Nations, and internationally coordinated efforts to separate FIFA from the world's biggest oil company Aramco, to fans of cycling, running and winter sports, a wave of activism is rising reminiscent of the uprising against big tobacco, but potentially even greater, given the supporter base of sport. Groups are coming together and organising through alliances like the Cool Down sport for climate action network.

But, as our writers show, sport is much more than a story machine.

It's a place where new communities are created and established communities come together.

When Tahir Shams approached the historic athletics club Herne Hill Harriers in South London's Tooting neighbourhood with the idea of creating a different kind of running club, open to those who may never have run at all, nobody foresaw that within a year hundreds of local people new to club running would weekly fill the athletics track and over a hundred each week join a social run around the nearby Common. And, it wasn't just that a lot of people were getting active, Tooting Run Club, as it became known, quickly won national awards for its outreach and creation of a free, supportive, nurturing community for the local area. Tooting Run Club is a hyper local twist on other phenomenally successful sports initiatives like Parkrun, the volunteer organised, weekly, timed 5k runs in mostly urban green spaces. Although some treat Parkrun like a competition, the appeal for many is social and its primary purpose was, and remains, not setting speed records, but bringing record numbers of people in a community together.

The benefits of sport for mental and general health are now so well appreciated that doctors' surgeries increasingly prescribe sport to treat a wide range of conditions.

For many, sport is also one of the few ways that people might have any contact with nature. The drivers of modern living isolate us into bubbles of passive consumerism. Sedentary lifestyles encouraged by car-biased transport systems that discourage walking and cycling, combine together with other modern addictions like screen time, fast food, home deliveries, and a long-hours, desk bound office culture.

Going for a run, a ride, an outdoor swim, a kickabout, football match or a tennis game may be among the few times that especially urban dwellers are reminded of the changing seasons, or touch grass, hear birdsong and be surrounded by trees.

Taking part in sport, put simply, is another way of being in the world, living a full, embodied life. It can tick all the boxes of the 'five ways to well-being: being active, connecting, keeping learning, taking notice and sharing. Sport does things to give you life-satisfaction that consumerism promises but fails to deliver. Local sport is exemplary in this regard, highlighting a tension with more global games.

Elite sport gets the vast majority of media attention, hype and money. Bold claims of 'inspiring a generation' and 'legacy' are common justifications for the public millions spent on elite events like the

Olympic Games.[1] The problem is that the evidence does not support such claims of an elite 'demonstration' effect driving local participation. Post the London Olympics the heralded legacy of a new, motivated generation failed to materialise.[2] Partly this is due to underfunding at the local level, and a failure to create the infrastructure needed, but also it is perhaps due to a more fundamental misunderstanding: a mismatch between the assumptions of elite sports' administrators and governing bodies and the practical realities of what people actually seek and can gain from sport, and how they go about it.

To get people running or walking around their local park at 9am on a Saturday morning, the promise of social contact, camaraderie, feedback, a sense of improving and belonging are key ingredients to the success of something like parkrun. Far fewer are likely motivated to get out of bed thinking they might emulate a distant Olympic gold medalist.

There seems to be a great imbalance in which the big bets to promote public benefit from sport are placed on the demonstration effect of the elite and

---

1   Leland *et al* (2019) Was Glasgow 2014 inspirational? Exploring the legacy impacts of a mega-sport event via the theorized demonstration and festival effects, Sport and Society https://www.tandfonline.com/doi/full/10.1080/17430437.2019.1571044#2b85d6ca-6520-4a3d-8e4a-aa-9f2ee3f33d-b6de7b7c-de82-45a5-9538-313dd15c6659

2   National Audit Office (2022) Grassroots Participation in Sport and Physical Activity https://www.nao.org.uk/reports/grassroots-participa-tion-in-sport-and-physical-activity/

international level. As if the sweat dripping from remote, hero-worshipped medal winners falls in magic drops to inspire all it touches. Whereas it tends to be the less glamorous, poorly funded, local level which, against the odds, has the track record of success. That doesn't mean there's anything wrong in enjoying the performance of elite athletes, it's just that if you want to widen and democratise the many benefits of sport, you need to look elsewhere, invest differently and create a more fertile soil at the grassroots. Otherwise that brilliant sweat falls on stony ground.

As many in this book argue, the pendulum has swung too far in favour of elite sport. Now, for the wide range of human benefits, and a more ecologically viable model for sport, it needs to swing back to the local. Their views are backed by the likes of Financial Times columnist and author of Soccernomics, Simon Kuper, who argues that our approach to sport is 'upside-down'.[3] "Why have we created a country that obsesses about Olympic medals, about the Premier League, about the England football manager, and yet nearly half the population gets no exercise at all. And most kids who want to be the next Vicky Pemberton (Olympic gold medal winning cyclist) or Wayne Rooney (England footballer) will never even get the chance to try." Paralympian Baroness Tanni Grey-Thompson, adds, "Unless we look more creatively

---

3   https://www.probonoeconomics.com/News/now-on-youtube-has-britain-got-sport-upside-down

about how we engage everyone in physical activity, we may win medals but we will be bottom of the league table on health and wellbeing."

The urban green spaces set aside for local sport (think of all the school playing fields tragically sold off for speculative speculative developments), and sports' physical infrastructure of community spaces to gather, play another potentially life saving role in an era of global heating.

Towns and cities with more trees and green spaces are less vulnerable to extreme weather events, whether those might be heatwaves or heavy rainfall. Too many hard, paved surfaces in urban areas create a 'heat island' effect – hotspots that are lethal to more vulnerable people. They reduce the ability for rainfall to be safely absorbed, exacerbating run-off and the likelihood of flooding as drainage systems become overwhelmed by sudden inundations.

As the public sphere in some countries like the UK has been heavily eroded over recent decades through privatisations, selling off public land and buildings, gated developments and the loss of school fields – local sports clubs provide a vital buffer. As networks of civil society, they are havens that not only deliver on their primary purpose of giving opportunities to participate in sport but are important community assets in times of need when public gathering spaces are needed. Where do people go when the flood comes or a wildfire levels their home? Usually it is the nearest school or sports hall. With society so widely unprepared for the worsening impacts of global heating this local infrastructure will be key to resilience – not just for shelter, but the networks and relationships they create and maintain within local areas.

A large and growing literature also points to both the huge mental health benefits of access to green space, and the great inequality of access to it. Increasing green urban spaces that can double as places for physical exercise can help dramatically improve physical and mental health.

Sport has vast potential to make lives better, but it can just as easily be harnessed for more toxic ends.

It is easy to forget that for all its pious veneration of sporting ideals, the modern Olympics was built on foundations that gloried in colonial domination, were explicitly sexist, divisive and class-based. Women and working class people were banned from its 'amateur' competition (the latter, extraordinarily, because their working lives involved physical labour that was paid). Its apparently ancient rituals are almost entirely modern inventions, from the torch procession infamously bequeathed by the Nazi's 1936 Olympics, to the podium, medals, and flag ceremonies. Today the Olympics might be stained by the sponsorship of major polluters, like in Paris 2024 the car company Toyota and airline Air France, both examples of industries that not only are major emitters of climate pollution, but who consistently obstruct and avoid climate action (in the run up to Paris news emerged that Toyota's reportedly huge, and much criticised,

$835 million Olympic deal might finally be ending). Yet the very fact that the event has moved on from some of its historical wrongs shows that change is possible. The challenge to this and other big global sporting competitions is to be on the side of life and a future for humanity. At the moment leadership is lacking in other major sports governance bodies, such as FIFA who offer themselves as billboards for some of the world's worst polluters, and are changing the game in ways that seem almost designed to maximise their damage – with bigger competitions spread across continents. New visions are needed and, in a very small way, this book hopefully adds something.

If a single, very personal, image can capture the essence of what sport can bring, for me it is caught in a photograph of my daughter, Scarlett, aged five, running across the long, dreary raised pedestrian walkway over the platforms of Clapham Junction railway station in London.

A late winter sun casts dramatic, long shadows on the ground. She is running fast towards me, so fast that in the picture she is blurred and almost bursts out of the frame. Exploding with joy, behind her there is a shrinking perspective of shadows that stretch into the distance. I look at this picture and experience a rush of thoughts: that we are born to run, that sport is just another word for play and can happen anywhere, that it is a celebration of life and a beautiful way to be in the world, and that this is one of the best stories sport can tell.

Sport Local for Life: a vision and practical opportunity

The time has come for us all to make a choice. This is the moment, you are either in or you're out. The window of opportunity to secure a liveable future for humanity is closing and we are on the verge of being shut on the wrong side – permanently and irreversibly.

What can sport do?
What has sport already done?

Global sport has and continues to accelerate the climate crisis. Mega sporting events are responsible for massive detrimental effects on the climate: transport, construction, unrecyclable materials, energy consumption, to name a few of sport's contributions to this disaster.

We are now seeing that sport is far from immune to climate change. Since 2019 at least, we have discovered that you cannot play rugby through a typhoon, nor tennis surrounded by fire and smoke, you can't run safely in 40 degree heat, you can't ski without snow, you can't play cricket underwater and you can't – no matter how much money you have – play football in Qatar during the summer.

Just imagine, for a moment, what we'll discover we can't do by 2070.

For starters. If we continue emitting as we are, in 2070 up to three billion people could be displaced because their homeland will be incapable of supporting livelihoods and therefore uninhabitable. Local sport will become a thing of the past for billions of people. Massive polluting competitions, such as the Olympics, will become harder and harder to justify as countries that should be competing are swallowed up by rising sea levels; torn apart by fires, floods, storms; ravaged by starvation and drought.

We are on the clock. Time is ticking.

But a choice was mentioned, and a choice is what we have.

Let's look at an alternative. And the best part is, it happens to be better than what we have now anyway.

Nelson Mandela once said, "Sport has the power to change the world, it has the power to excite, it has the power to unite"

Here is an invitation to unite with those who believe that the change now needed is to make sport local. To help make that happen I set up *Sport Local for Life* (sport-local.earth). It is here to reconnect sport with the grassroots values of participation, wellbeing and joy. We aim to help communities rediscover the immense benefits of local-level sport: building friendships, creating local heroes, opportunities to shine, improving physical and mental health, connecting societies and protecting natural environments. This is what sport should be about.

Sport Local for Life is a vision of a clear-eyed and inspirational emergency response to this environmental crisis to both encourage and create positive change, while embracing the responsibility that comes with sport's huge reach and power.

But how do we do this? There are six simple steps. First, the challenge is to shift resources and funding from large national and international competitions to which there is a conventional funding bias, but that cannot function sustainably, and redirect them more towards local clubs and competitions, where additional community benefits are also easier to deliver.

Second, the target is to select local, national and regional venues that can be reached by public transport to host these competitions. These venues should be zero emission or be genuinely committed to shifting to zero emission on site, with plans of action and clear timeframes.

Third, we create sport fan hubs for enjoying sporting events in communal locations that are accessible by active and public transport. Still supporting travel to live, in-person events when it is possible to do so using public transport.

Fourth will be to refocus the international sporting calendar to only pinnacle events, minimising the impact of international competition schedules.

Fifth, alongside the rest of society and the economy, we move into a rapid emergency mode for the decarbonisation of existing sporting infrastructure, restore and protect nature on sports grounds and in surrounding areas.

Lastly, because this will be a dynamic, ongoing and long term transition, we can form sporting imaginariums where we envision local solutions, to create a sustainable future for sport together.

Sport Local for Life would bring more sport to more people, increasing mental, physical and community health and at the same time demonstrate that tackling the climate and ecological emergency will bring many benefits. Sport Local for Life seeks to embody a desire for people in the future to enjoy sport in the way it is supposed to be enjoyed, as well as for protecting all life on earth.

This initiative can be about your team, your club, your country and your planet. To take up the call and participate in every way you can. We don't yet know what Sport Local for Life looks like at your club, but we want to give you the power to make changes. So you can imagine it. Believe in it, and make it happen.

Change is inevitable, we either change decisively or destructively. By choice or by force of nature. Right now we have a choice, yes. But choice, don't forget, is a luxury. It's a luxury we have now, and which we may not have in another five or ten years' time. For the sustainable future of sport, and for the future of the planet, we can choose Sport Local for Life.

Two visions

Sport local – a vision for 2030

Laura Baldwin, Olympic sailor

In 2030 we'll either be fully engaged in positive transformative adaptation or we'll have missed the narrow window of opportunity to secure a liveable world. If we messed up, then we would be managing the effects of our crazy climate causing the collapse of our food and fresh water systems, our ecological and our social systems. My heart aches at the thought so I switch my focus.

Rob Hopkins, co-founder of the Transition Network, makes living sustainably sound tantalising and irresistible. He dresses in a spacesuit and holds up a sign that reads,

'I've been to the future, and we won!' I find that especially powerful.

So when I receive the invitation to go in Rob's spaceship (in fact a podcast) to 2030, together with Sky Sports Presenter, David Garrido, of course I leap at the opportunity, buzzing at the chance. I gave myself time to daydream, to come up with my most imaginative and desirable vision for how good things could be, if we gave it everything between now and then.

So, here we are, we arrived in 2030. Whilst David went straight off to a football match to see how things have changed. I hopped on a bike and cycled around the local area.

I am so thrilled to see what I am seeing and hearing. People are noticeably happier and they all look fit and healthy. Their eyes sparkle as they speak. I notice how fresh the air smells. It is clean with frequent pockets of wonderful aromas from flowers. The perfumes hit my senses with delight. A feeling that is intensifying as I see how thoughtfully the area has been returned to nature and repurposed for people.

There are no cars packed in the residential streets, in their place I'm seeing all kinds of different uses. I love how much communal space there is now for neighbours to sit outside and eat and chat together, with plants and trees in every suitable location. There are bike storage boxes that double as climbing walls with cubby houses on top for the kids to play and zip lines between them, others are covered in living walls with beautiful wildflowers on top. Outdoor play and fitness equipment is found on every street.

Efficient public transport, electric rail, trams, buses and taxis have removed the need for privately owned cars, reduced individual cost and eliminated stress as roads are no longer congested or polluted. I've seen all kinds of incredibly creative uses for cargo bikes with trailers for mobile market stalls, caterers, trades people and delivery riders zipping around with boxes piled high along with most other people who are riding around the safe cycle networks. There's also this super smooth path for skating and scooting at top speeds that looks so much fun! It's covered with a roof of solar panels.

Solar panels can be seen on all the roofs. People's homes are well insulated and temperature controlled. There are only patches of grass where there is play equipment, sports grounds, picnic areas and paths, for the rest is growing food or providing habitat for nature.

I've had a few chats with people that I've met and they told me that it was sport that led the way in making the changes happen. Sports – so often an almost invisible presence at the heart of every community, chose to showcase the needed actions in exciting, appealing and rewarding ways. Using billboards and pitch sides to advertise sustainable lifestyles rather than cars, airlines, fossil fuel companies and gambling firms.

Slogans and posters on leisure centre walls reached everyday people in all different communities. Sports stars acted as role models, sharing their carbon reduction journeys and bringing people along with them. Sharing the qualities of the athlete mindset. Everyone got onboard incredibly quickly as they could clearly see that this was desirable. They felt a deep sense of purpose in finding their role in the transition and they are brimming with pride sharing all the contributions that they had made.

Sports fan hubs are some of the most attractive local social places to hang out. Broadcasting sporting events on big screens when major events are happening and they are even used for the community to get together to enjoy watching the best in their towns compete to be the local sporting heroes as not everyone can see it happening inside the venues. Communities have connected and bonded stronger than ever before with sport helping to excite and unite across social divides.

There's been a huge refocus around food, everything is plant based, people are cooking communally, it's been a really strong connecting force. Learning to make veggies taste delicious, sharing skills and flavours. People have realised that fresh, locally grown, organic food really is medicine and a joyful experience.

Sport is a major factor in everybody's lives thanks to the ditching of GDP for assessing success. I am so happy that they ditched GDP! And instead they bought in NHI, a National Happy Planet Index, a measure developed by the UK based New Economics Foundation, where success is measured on the long, happy lives of their citizens achieved with minimal impact on nature. And everyone I've met really does seem so happy and fulfilled with their lives.

There has been a re-localisation for sports, boosting opportunities for everyone to participate in different sports. Focusing back to the grassroots joy of participation and improved wellbeing. It's more about challenging yourself, bettering your skills and dabbling in all kinds of different sports than about being really good at one thing. There are still people that choose to go that route and they travel to international competitions by public transport that has become far more accessible and reliable and, most adventurously, there has been a huge upsurge in people travelling by sailboat.

Aviation had to be grounded and initially people were shocked and angry, but sport really helped by using its power of communication to show people that pausing pollution to await solutions was essential and how positive this pause could be, how it could improve everyone's quality of life. Through sport, people were called to set goals that excite them, that motivated them to get on with making positive changes happen.

Everyone seems to have a strong sense of purpose. There's much less of a feeling of a need to escape their lives. Though travel is still widely experienced, there isn't such a need to go so far because every town has a unique character. Filled with independent shops and cafes, upcycled clothing and furniture stores, locally made arts and crafts, specialist repair cafes and loads of cool sports to enjoy.

Green Gyms are the hippest thing to be involved in, combining exercise with restoring nature, planting trees and re-wilding suitable sections of land held by sports clubs and then taking these skills and spreading the good work out into the local area.

Kids have reclaimed the streets, they are playing, cycling, scooting, making dens and climbing trees. What I can hear, now the noise of traffic has dimmed, is people chatting, the cheers of excitement, encouraging each other on. There's both a serene sense of calm but also a high energy, a buzz about the place. I really like it here, can I stay?

Knowing that the solutions do already exist and simply need scaling up and rolling out at speed makes me feel hopeful that this vision could come to life. If sport will realise its power and step up to the challenge in this, the race for our lives.

A day in the life of a professional player in 2030
Joe Hodge

Sport has changed so much since I was growing up. As a young athlete, I never imagined I would make it to this level. I also never thought sport would be the way it is today. I watched the World Cup as a child thinking 'I want to be there in that big fancy stadium', but it somehow felt so far away.

Both from where I was living and from my own experience of football. Those athletes on TV had everything they could want: equipment, money, adoration, support... but where I was, we had none of that. Where we are now is so much better and it feels even better knowing it's here to stay.

When I was a child, the climate emergency was a big thing. It was all over the news and while I didn't fully understand what was happening, I knew we all had to change so I could carry on playing the sport I love. I was afraid that I wouldn't make it to the World Cup, and I was also afraid that it wouldn't even exist when I grew up. The sporting events I watched on TV were everything, they gave me the motivation and inspiration to say: that's my calling, that's where I want to be. So I was afraid that would be taken away. But here we are, and it is just magical.

I have never felt healthier. Since taking up a more plant-based diet, I feel so much happier and healthier knowing my body is fueled and I'm doing good for the planet. Everything we need is around us, we just need to open our eyes and look for it.

I now have so much more space and time to get out into the community. I never had this as a child because I only ever saw athletes through a TV screen. They were still inspirational, but if I had the chance to speak to them like I speak to my community, perhaps these changes could have come sooner? Who knows.

The streets leading to the stadium are vibrant and bustling, reflecting the sustainable transport priorities of our community. Smooth surfaces, designed specifically for cycling, skating, or scootering, guide me to the heart of our local sporting hub. It's exhilarating to see families and fellow sports enthusiasts taking to these car-free roads, embracing active modes of transportation.

Upon reaching the stadium, I am greeted by the sound of cheers and the warm camaraderie of the local community. The once-empty spaces surrounding the stadium have been transformed into lush green areas, seamlessly blending nature into the urban landscape. This harmonious coexistence with nature is a constant reminder of our commitment to sustainability and the well-being of our planet.

Training sessions are filled with determination and a shared passion for the beautiful game. As I step onto the immaculate pitch, the energy in the air is palpable. Our training facilities are state-of-the-art, equipped with cutting-edge technology and resources that empower us to hone our skills.

I get unwavering support from my local community. The stands are packed with enthusiastic fans, friends, and families who come together to cheer us on. The atmosphere is electric, and I always feel that fire within me to perform at my best and inspire the next generation of aspiring football players.

Our community's commitment to sports is reflected in the incredible network of sports clubs that have become integral parts of our lives. These clubs are more than just places to train; they are vibrant hubs where families and friends gather, strengthening the bonds that tie our community together. The support we receive from coaches, teammates, and fellow club members fuels our determination to succeed.

Beyond the training grounds and match days, the local community plays an active role in supporting our journey. Whether it's through local sponsorships, fundraisers, or simply showing up to cheer us on, their presence and encouragement propel us forward. The solidarity we feel is immeasurable, reinforcing the belief that we are not just individual players, but representatives of a united community.

In this transformed sporting landscape, the concept of competition has taken on a new meaning.

While the desire to win still exists, the emphasis has shifted towards personal growth, self- improvement, and collective achievement. We are encouraged to push our limits, embrace teamwork, and strive for excellence both on and off the field.

As a football player in 2030, I am grateful to be part of a world that values and supports sports at the local level. The journey to this point has been transformative, with our community's dedication to sustainability, inclusivity, and well-being shaping every aspect of our sporting experience.

We have a beautiful world of sport now, it's green, it's safe and we can make the most of what this world was really meant to be.

How globalised sport's race to the bottom can become a recovery run

Benjamin Mole

Ellis Park Stadium in downtown Johannesburg is one of the most iconic stadiums in sport. It witnessed Nelson Mandela holding the Rugby World Cup trophy aloft in a moment that, at least for a while, helped heal a nation from the deepest of wounds. That day in 1995 saw the stadium packed to its 65,000 capacity. The stadium would still be at capacity the following year for the final of the Currie Cup, the oldest national rugby competition in the world. For those fans, their club was something unique to them, a symbol of their city and their way of life.

Now that club, officially named the Emirates Lions, plays in an international league with sides from Europe called the United Rugby Championship (URC). In early 2023, as the Lions take to the field, Ellis Park barely gets 11,000 supporters. The traditions of *braais* and *bakkies* outside the stadium (the South African equivalent of tailgating) are no more. The clubs of the URC fly 12,000km back and forth across the equator multiple times per year, with the corresponding climate-polluting aviation emissions, bringing almost no travelling fans. This is unsustainable.

In contrast, the number of South Africans flying 10 hours each way to the UK every year to watch football games is increasing. The English Premier League (EPL) is arguably the biggest domestic sports league in the world and, while efforts in stadiums to go fully solar and collect wastewater are admirable, the elephant in the room are those 'scope 3 emissions': the vast number of fans travelling to venues across continents.[4] No low carbon travel option is available over these distances within the timeframe available to fight catastrophic climate change. This is also unsustainable. What is happening?

Push and pull

To start, why did the South African rugby clubs join a European league? Although it is easy to cast them as greedy, the former Pro14 clubs and the biggest club sides in South Africa would both argue that they

---

4   So-called Scope 3 emissions are the result of activities not owned or controlled by the polluter in question, but happen as a result of what that group, company or event does. Hence, in this example, if sports leagues or teams organise an event which is intended for the public to attend, the emissions that result from the public travelling to that event are the club or events 'scope 3' emissions.

needed to increase their revenues as they were losing players to the English, French and Japanese leagues where there is no salary cap and a stronger currency. Indeed, this new tournament was a pivot from a similar manoeuvre when in 2016 Super Rugby had expanded from Australian, New Zealand and South African clubs to include one from Argentina and one from Japan. Super Rugby itself was only a 25-year-old tournament that had internationalised club rugby across the Southern hemisphere. These globalising manoeuvres are getting more frequent, and all of them have seemingly failed to stop interest dwindling.

What is gaining interest is EPL football. Its rise in South Africa, and around the world, has been unprecedented in recent decades, with many push and pull factors to dissect. On the push side, in South Africa watching sport on TV has become more popular in part due to very poor transport infrastructure and significant safety issues. Most people with enough disposable income to spend on sport choose to live in American-styled sprawling suburbs (as land is relatively cheap) surrounded by massive walls. This was my childhood. I never missed a Lions game on TV, but it was a huge ask of my parents to get me to the stadium, in the same city but almost two hours away by car. As all Premier League games were available on that same TV, my family's historic fondness for Liverpool FC was greatly amplified. While these homes are spacious and comfortable, they make sowing the tight-knit fabric of a local community almost impossible. There is so little that brings people together; something that sport may have done in the past. Additionally, South Africa's macroeconomic situation cannot be ignored. Many citizens, including rugby players, are looking for greener pastures elsewhere and they take assets and expertise, but also local passions and interests, with them.

On the pull side, it is argued that the EPL product is 'better'. It is true that sports or teams with the most resources can buy the best players, scouts, coaches, physios and marketeers to win the most trophies and make the most money to be reinvested. Furthermore, these tight-knit sporting communities singing arm-in-arm in the stands of European football do not go unnoticed by South Africans watching on TV. If it is almost impossible to create one's own sporting culture, the next best option is to join someone else's, and the giant European football clubs and leagues are playing a proactive role in this shift.

Despite their success, they know they are in a competitive market, so they are reinvesting their considerable resources into 'onboarding' overseas fans. It is not a huge stretch to compare this to a neo-colonial narrative, where clubs want to extract fans' attention and purchasing power. While this used to be mainly achieved with a pre-season tour, the role of social media cannot be understated. It is an exceptionally powerful feedback loop where continuous, attractive content leads to more people following a team and then many of the new fans start creating digital content of their own. This attracts more viewers and, most importantly, attracts advertisers, the proceeds of which can be reinvested in getting more people to support the team. As of 2023, such digital revenues started to outstrip matchday income, and the top clubs are some of the biggest businesses in the world. I recently heard directly from representatives of top European sides that their strategy now is to become media companies, with a strong brand to drive the purchases of more retail items and anything sellable that comes along, such as NFTs. And if local fans grow tired of this barrage of consumption, advertisers aim their efforts at new fans overseas who are not yet so disillusioned.

Engagement is not enjoyment

While it can be nice to walk into almost any bar in the world and meet someone who supports a team you know, all is not well. Researchers found that the subjective well-being garnered from spectator sports diminishes when watching only on TV and particularly watching alone.[5] Furthermore, social media engagement is not necessarily positive engagement e.g., vehemently abusing other teams and fans still counts. Simply put, talking with friends and loved ones

---

5   Kim, J., & James, J. D. (2019). Sport and happiness: Understanding the re-
    lations among sport consumption activities, long-and short-term subjective
    well-being, and psychological need fulfillment. Journal of Sport Manage-
    ment, 33(2), 119-132.

about a shared community experience that the highs and lows of sport provide, is hard to replicate in the long term when the sport is happening very far away.

Bigger than sport – attention as a resource

Is this just an issue within sport? Certainly not. For example, the British economy has been struggling for years, most apparently since the Brexit vote. As its influence as the seat of a former vast empire continues to dwindle, it is left trying to grab whatever resources it can. Therefore it is seeking new avenues for influence and income. This is evident in how the British government helped push through the deal for the Saudi investment in Newcastle United, despite the obvious issues with fossil fuels and human rights abuses.[6] The EPL's traditions and culture are a commodity to mine like any other, in the same way, South Africa wants to attract tourists to its sunny beaches and game parks.

Similarly, is it just football that takes advantage of ever more individualistic communities? On the contrary, anything that can use significant resources to break into the attention economy makes it harder to keep traditions standing. Sport-loving parents are

---

6   Kim, J., & James, J. D. (2019). Sport and happiness: Understanding the relations among sport consumption activities, long-and short-term subjective well-being, and psychological need fulfillment. Journal of Sport Management, 33(2), 119-132.

put in an impossible situation where watching 80 minutes of rugby simply does not result in the same dopamine rise in their kids compared to Mr Beast compilations on TikTok. They are resented for taking away that high and replacing it with something that is now, by comparison, boring – even though in the past it was the highlight of the weekend.

The advertisement-supported media model, where maximum attention equals money, means that everyone and everything is drawn into an arms race of creating enticing content, whether they like it or not. Every inch of attention is squeezed out of as many people as possible until the unique cultures being sold collapse and actual local community bonds are broken. We become more cosmopolitan but less diverse. Not everyone can attend a Real Madrid game (without significant cost and/or emissions). And to be at home, maybe alone, left wanting something you cannot fully access, is perhaps worse than attending a smaller, less glamorous event. Likewise, although time on one's smartphone with the potent algorithms will be more entertaining than a full-length sports game, the long-term society-wide negative impacts are stacking up.

Moloch

This hints at a much bigger problem. Something akin to a global prisoner's dilemma or continuous multipolar traps, where the actions of individual actors (be they clubs, sports, corporations, tech developers etc.) lead to immense individual short-term gain with collective long-term consequences. Many have noticed this phenomenon across different fields, but it is perhaps best conceptualised by Scott Alexander's 'Meditations on Moloch' (2014). In it, he refers to the demon Moloch as the driver of that urge within us for short-term individual gain, condemning the system to a broader worse outcome. The Moloch metaphor does not imply an inner evil within us but rather a repeating outcome across large populations. While this short-term gain mindset may be evolutionary, Daniel Schmachtenberger argues that smaller tribal communities were able to keep it in check.[7] If an individual wronged someone or their actions harmed the group, everyone knew and there would be a reckoning and possible retribution. Today, in a complex, interconnected world of eight billion people, the well-meaning choice of a coder in Silicon Valley can have massive consequences for teenagers around the world, and we are left debating who is to blame.

Regulation

How do we solve this problem? Regulation may appear as the obvious choice but the *what* and *where* and *how* make it seem near impossible. Do we

---

7   Fridman, L (2022) Daniel Schmachtenberger: Steering Civilization Away from Self-Destruction | Lex Fridman Podcast #191, Available at: https://www.youtube.com/watch?v=hGRNUw559SE&pp=ygUXRGFuaWVsIFNjaG1hY2h0ZW5iZXJnZXI%3D

regulate other sports to not market to rugby fans, so that local rugby clubs can continue to thrive? Do we stipulate that town planners make sports stadiums accessible, even though current evidence implies that they won't get used because we are all on TikTok? Do we regulate social media companies? Well... YES, but their power is so significant that they can lobby their way out. It is challenging to go much higher than the nation-state policy as even nation-states are currently involved in their own arms races around AI technology and... arms. So, what hope do the rest of us have? Nevertheless, some argue that more appropriate use of new technologies will help, but this requires complete stakeholder buy-in as even a private individual acting in their own self-interest can gain that advantage. Easier said than done and, once again, it becomes a challenge to clearly communicate and coordinate.

Individual action as a collective solution

While regulation should be the primary action, its difficulty combined with the trajectory of sport as a globalised capitalist industry may now have you feeling pessimistic. But fortunately, there are two things that can bring hope.

Firstly, at least in team sports, over time the constant winner-takes-all can make things boring for fans. Researchers indicate that one or two teams winning all the time diminishes enjoyment in the league, particularly in the long term.[8] This is often seen in Formula One where, in the past decade, very few championships have been close. Years where a single car breaks records with absolute performance are simply not that enjoyable. The drama of multiple cars battling it out until the final corner of the final race is what makes it fun, and Formula One have been attempting to regulate teams to achieve this.

Secondly, once so much of the culture of a club has been commodified (often referred to as the Disneyfication), some fans turn away from a league but do not give up on sport. Indeed, some seek more local teams or less popular sports where their more central and valued role can be re-established. But again, lack of communication and coordination, even at the local level, is preventing more people from knowing this. People do not know that local options exist (as they don't trend on social media as readily) and that feelings of belonging and meaning can still be found closer to home. I tested this theory in recent years by volunteering with a fourth division women's football team. Even though none of the players on the pitch are as fast as Erling Haaland or Kylian Mbappé, the enjoyment of sport is inherent in competition. After time is invested to learn the team's narratives and establish relationships with

8   Manasis, V. & Ntzoufras, I. (2014). Between-seasons competitive balance in European football: review of existing and development of specially designed indices. Journal of Quantitative Analysis in Sports, 10(2), 139-152. https://doi.org/10.1515/jqas-2013-0107

fellow attendees, that feeling of belonging can emerge again.

What does the future look like?

Of course, it would be naive of me to hope that all teams will only be supported by their local village. I do not want to be overly nostalgic. If the technology is invented, it will be used. But the objectives can change, and the technology will follow. There is a vision of a world where, for example, South Africans build mighty sporting institutions of their own, providing a compelling reason for people to remain there. Such institutions can inform local planning and infrastructure to make games accessible to all in the area. Leagues can be built within more realistic distances requiring far less carbon to traverse. Maybe football or games that are yet to be invented are inherently more interesting than rugby and that is fine. But the problems highlighted in this article should stand as a guide on how to build the next sporting ecosystem. Africa's footballing institutions are attempting to grow, but are currently growing within the European Champions League model, with huge distances between venues and oil company sponsorships that are bleeding resources off the continent. Instead, what if the primary goal of a sports team was to maximise the well-being and joy of its local supporters, and not just to have as many monetisable supporters as possible? This would provide a much-needed sense of community and identity to thousands if not millions of people.

This vision might seem to border on the delusional as it requires total stakeholder buy-in, from the club level all the way to the biggest tech companies and anyone trying to create entertainment. It's a tough ask, saying to FC Barcelona's social media team, 'Stop what you are doing' and accept that their revenues will decrease. Such stepping down of production has been called for in other industries by the post-growth and degrowth movements. Rarely has entertainment and culture been at the centre of that debate.

But based on the logic of avoiding a race to the bottom both in terms of well-being and the emissions expelled on the way down, there is a strong case that we collectively take our foot off the gas. Then we need to identify what elements of sport are important to us, with the aim of maximising well-being for the greatest number of people and coordinating some kind of emergent system where no one's short-term gain puts the collective – society as a whole – at risk.

This coordination will be difficult as there are many perspectives that need a voice. I like to imagine my hometown of Johannesburg as one where sports venues bring people of the city's multiple creeds and backgrounds together, outside digital spaces. The joy and novelty are in how games unfold, something that has kept people collectively enthralled for decades. Smaller doesn't seem so bad when everybody there knows your name and they are always glad you came.

Cheating

Nicky Saunter

During lockdown, as our family came together on Zoom for Sunday evenings of chat and the occasional quiz, someone suggested a family slideshow. As the family photographer, I have possession of the archive – a series of beautiful purpose-made boxes containing slides from the early 1960s to the 1980s taken by my father, and then my own additions through to the 1990s. During those long evenings at home in the early months of the pandemic, I bought a cheap if laborious single-slot scanner and digitised the whole lot with the plan of doing regular online Sunday evening slideshows.

The results were somehow in keeping with the strong colours of old Kodachrome, the tiny floating creatures of dust and scratches on the emulsion surface. We danced and grinned across the years, adding a child here, losing an older relative there. One slide caught my eye and took me right back to the moment it was taken.

The image shows children at the finishing tape of

some strange kind of race. There are lines painted on the grass and the young competitors are frozen in a crouching position known as the bunnyhop – and they are wearing an unusual array of badly fitting clothes. I realised with a jolt of recognition, seeing the swing of familiar heavy brown hair, that the child approaching the finish line is me, head down, earnestly bunnyhopping my heart away. To my left a boy is already standing up, his humiliating bunny-hopping stance no longer needed. He is wearing a dress that may be on back to front and I know that he is called Paul. Above us, I can see from the adult angle of my photographer father (although I have no memory of him being there) several teachers are looking down on us, laughing.

We look funny and cute, but it didn't feel that way. The obstacle race was well crafted, with a mix of skills giving children of different abilities the chance to shine. I remember threading beads onto a string (easy), drinking a glass of water (hard – I can only do mouthfuls), jumping in a sack (fun), carrying an egg on a spoon (easy), putting on an article of clothing (this felt somehow humiliating even then) and then the final bunny hop to glory. This was an awkward move, especially in a lady's nightie, but it was important to follow the rules – feet together, then hands, feet, then hands. It was only in the last few moments as I looked up through the curtain of obscuring hair that I saw Paul blatantly running on his hands and feet. He was cheating. It felt serious, stinging and unfair.

Laboriously crossing the line in second place, I realised nothing would happen to Paul. What he had done was funny and no one minded and he was awarded first place. But I minded. Was it indignation at his cheating blatantly and getting away with it or my embarrassment at seeing how they were all laughing at my immaculate rule-following bunny hop?

Paul and I competed often at school, vying for the top spot in various areas, but this felt different. He had changed the rules and people had not only let him; they had joined him in laughing at his success. To complain or be miserable would be churlish but it was definitely how I felt. What was the lesson from this – that cheating sometimes pays? That to buck the system can reap benefits? Or that boys win and girls come second?

Looking back I can see there is a time when primary school sport reaches a magical balancing point at which girls and boys abilities can be similar. Boys have not yet gained their extra muscle and girls have not had their range of movement shrunken by society's expectations. Our rounders team was mixed, although there was no such word; it was just the rounders team. We cycled together, boys and girls taking turns to slipstream for each other, on long rides along dusty country lanes. On a meadow by the church we played football, jumpers for goalposts, no referee, lots of laughing and shouting. At the old mill pond we swam and dived down to touch the twisted tree roots, scaring each other witless with tales of giant lurking pike or sunken dead bodies. It probably only lasted a few years, but it was glorious.

All this from a single slide. Stimulated by a global pandemic that ripped our previous world away and forced us to make up a new one, where those of us with families and the means to communicate with them started new ways of talking to each other. Some of these new ways of meeting have stuck, with online and social network groups forming for social, political, work and sporting reasons. Perhaps I could start one for adults to relearn how we did it as children – before the world and then hormones forced us apart – when we played together for the sheer joy of it.

Running Out Of Excuses?

Damian Hall

Sports activists are caught in a climate crossfire, but have so much potential to score system-change goals. I am a climate activist (I've got an appropriately offbeat/wacky haircut and everything). But I will fly from the UK to America in 2024 to run around in some woods for a bit. Because I'm also an elite athlete (just about).

I'm really anxious about our climate and ecological emergency. But I still want to be a competitive ultramarathon runner, so I'll be adding two tonnes of CO_2e to my personal footprint, for what may sound to some like a pointless or frivolous reason and naturally brands me a hypocrite to tabloid newspapers and keyboard commandos. It's at best a somewhat conflicting and at worst a deeply uncomfortably compromising and angsty position to be in.

The Barkley Marathons is a really special, unique, even exclusive event, at the top of my bucket list, and I dearly wish I could get there in a feasible lower-carbon way. At 48, I'm clinging desperately to the label of elite sportsperson, namely an ultramarathon runner who's represented Great Britain. I've reduced my own footprint all I realistically can (I use the Eco setting on my dishwasher and everything), but I only have a few years left to attempt these amazing adventures. Which also support my family.

My flight isn't necessary. But is it reasonable? Some will think so. Some won't. I used to fly three times a year for running but have reduced that to twice in five years. A few athletes do even better than that. Some tell me to stop fretting about my personal footprint when I feel I'm doing all I can elsewhere. Plus there's the eternal debate about how significant our personal footprint is anyway, when one percent of super emitters create more CO_2e than the bottom 66 percent (and take 50 percent of the flights) and the concept was dreamed up by a PR firm employed by BP.

For most elite sports, competition is international and flying is commonplace. But there's more harm done. Travel isn't cheap, so being sponsored can really help, and that usually comes from a sports brand. In turn, not unreasonably, the brand expects an athlete they support to return the favour by bigging them up on social media and in interviews. But that's fresh oxygen to the flames of overconsumption and no industry does overconsumption quite like the running-shoe industry, where 99 percent of products are made from oil and we're constantly told a new super-duper-shoe will make us a faster, better athlete.

Runners are also encouraged to consume ample protein to aid muscle recovery, which in most cases comes from the meat and dairy industry, responsible for 14 percent of global emissions.

Sport is a huge part of the Big Kerfufflefuck. Its emissions have been calculated to be somewhere between that of Bolivia and Poland. Professor Mike Berners-Lee estimates that outside of war, the 2022 football World Cup in Qatar was the biggest single human-made carbon event ever. The Olympic Games can't be much better. Sport is so great. But so terrible. But also could be very, very helpful in scoring some system-change goals.

Ignorance was bliss. I felt better about my life before my red or blue pill, Matrix moment. When I was oblivious to the harm that international sport, my sport of trail-ultramarathon running and my own personal actions contribute towards climate breakdown. Since being woken (pun intended) up by Extinction Rebellion in 2019, I've massively reduced my personal footprint. As well as reducing flying, I've turned Full Annoying Vegan and reached a better agreement with my primary sponsor, where I promote them only under certain conditions (I love to when they make sustainability wins), essentially much less often.

I've done all I can think of to cut my personal footprint. I've said no thanks to numerous appealing events, in the Himalayas, Mexico, Japan. I've taken multi-day bus-and-coach journeys across Europe to races instead of flying, with all the delays and mishaps you'd expect, and sometimes subsequent sub-par performances. I've decided not to ever do several high-profile races, because they'd realistically require a flight. And boycotted races with high-carbon sponsors, including our sport's biggest event, UTMB Mont-Blanc. I've stopped working with four sponsors because I didn't feel they were taking our global crisis seriously (it doesn't take two years to write a sustainability policy). I'm in the habit of unfurling a Just Stop Oil flag at finish lines, to mixed reactions (heehee).

Personal actions are important, of course. But Big Oil is the footprint we should all be scrutinising and why it is that governments seem so reluctant to tackle the oil rig in the room. Nudging the system has potentially far more impact. I've joined numerous protests, with Extinction Rebellion and the ace folk at Champions 4 Earth. In early 2022, with around 10 other climate concerned folk, I co-founded The Green Runners, which now has well over 1,000 members, was nominated for a 2023 BBC Green Sport Award and has had some relative success in anti-sportswashing campaigns. I wrote a book, We Can't Run Away From This. Dr and author Katharine Hayhoe says the most important thing we can do is talk about 'it' and I've done that in over 50 interviews in just a few months of this year.

I've used all the influence I can think of to nudge for system change. Yet I book a flight as a sportsperson, and I feel effing awful about it. Like it's undoing everything else I've done.

It doesn't seem fair for sportspeople to be caught in a climate crossfire. It doesn't seem fair that high-carbon industries use sport to try and distract us from their crimes, either. Sportswashing is becoming horribly prevalent, with at least 250 cases to date.

I really admire the young runner Innes Fitzgerald for not taking a flight to Australia for the World Cross Country Championships, and my friends Jasmin Paris and Andy Symonds for saying no to GB selection in 2022, because the World Trail Championships were in Thailand. I admire Australian cricketer Pat Cummins, F1 driver Sebastian Vettel, Danish footballer Sofie Junge Pedersen even more, though, because although they're involved in high-carbon sports, they're not afraid to speak up, despite knowing they'll be lazily branded hypocrites. That's what keeps so many other sportspeople quiet.

It's also useful to show that activists don't have to be perfect. In fact, they can't be anyway, as we'll all have some kind of CO_2e footprint. Hopefully that also helps open the door for people who care a bit but who also really like beef burgers. If those who speak up are only flight-dodging vegans in second-hand clothes, we're unlikely to enlist the masses.

I know elite runners who care and make really conscientious travel and sponsorship decisions, but don't talk publicly about them. EcoAthletes tell me that the fear they have of being branded a hypocrite

– as well as it being seen as "too sciencey" or "too political" – are the main reasons they don't speak up. Yet research shows that it is sportspeople, not actors, musicians or politicians, who are the most influential people of our time. They could have so much influence. But so many remain quiet. Some kind of carbon budget for elite sportspeople could be really helpful?

More athletes will speak up. Because climate breakdown is affecting sport massively. F1 races and football matches are being cancelled due to flooding, cricket games are called off due to wildfires and air pollution, future Winter Olympic Games are in question. Three-quarters of athletes have been directly impacted by climate change, with 85 percent saying sport has suffered because of it, according to a World Athletics survey.

Sport is at the forefront of climate breakdown and nothing has global reach like it. Music, film or most news events don't come close for getting people together, all watching and talking about the same thing. That's a powerful platform. The most powerful one. And why we must keep high-carbon-sponsors out and give athletes the oxygen they need to breathe. And speak up.

The Alternative Games

Geoff Mead

Secretary-General J-C Beauregard
International Alternative Olympic Association
Lausanne, Switzerland
1st January 2016

Dear Sir

In support of our candidacy to host the 2028 Alternative Olympics, I am writing to confirm the commitment of the Lower Wallop Alternative Olympics Association (LWAOA) to meet, and indeed exceed, the principles established by the United Nations Sports for Climate Action Framework. Rather than speak in vague generalities that merely express good intentions, as we believe other candidates may have done, I shall enumerate the concrete steps we have taken to adjust the rules for specific alternative sports, and for the construction of appropriate venues, etc.

Shin Kicking

An English sport dating back to the 16th Century. Boots to be handcrafted from vegan leather substitute. Hobnails to be forged from reclaimed metal by local blacksmiths. All shin guards to be padded only with organically certified, locally grown straw.

Hill Running

To be run on the spot, barefoot, thus avoiding the possibility both of damage to alpine wildflowers and the importation of sweatshop-manufactured running shoes. Competitors will be judged on the basis of endurance (last one standing) rather than speed over a course.

Spurning the Barre

A little-known rural sport akin to Tossing the Caber. Barres will be exclusively selected from naturally fallen trees within a 5-mile radius of the arena. Off-cuts and chippings will be burnt as biomass for the Alternative Olympic Flame.

Tug of War

We are mainly concerned by the bellicose nature of this event. Henceforth, teams will work in tandem to pull cars stuck in the mud onto dry ground. This only applies in the event of heavy rain (which always seems to happen during summertime in Lower Wallop).

Fireball Soccer

The practice of setting fire to a kerosene-soaked ball will cease immediately. We are currently sourcing a net-zero, solar-powered, LED substitute, which, though not quite as dramatic as a flaming football, will reduce CO_2 emissions and save many injuries.

Gurning

The ancient art of face-pulling presents no obvious problems apart from the use of mass-produced horse-collars. Organisers will provide a single antique horse-collar to be used by all competitors. Excessive dental extractions for unfair advantage will lead to disqualification.

Extreme Ironing

The use of drip-dry items of clothing will be encouraged to save electricity. Travel to exotic locations is banned, competitors being judged instead on ironing style, fashion-sense, and the imaginative use of starch substitutes. We are also happy to announce the advent of Synchronised Extreme Ironing.

Wife Carrying

The issue here is one of gender equality rather than environmental impact. There is no place for so-called Culture Wars in the Games. So, like some equestrian events, the sport is now unisex and has been renamed Spouse/Civil Partner/Just Good Friends Carrying.

Pooh Sticks

Certification that the stick has been crafted from either native or non-invasive imported plant growth, will ensure that there is no long-term detrimental impact on local flora and fauna. All sticks must be recovered after judging, dried, and used as biomass (see also, Spurning the Barre).

Ferret Legging

Always popular with spectators, this endurance sport has been accused of cruelty (both to ferrets and competitors). In future, all parties – mustelidae and human – will be required to sign declarations of voluntary participation.

Worm Charming

We regret to inform you that this event will no longer form part of the Alternative Olympics as we have been unable to locate any site in Lower Wallop with a sufficient population of worms for a viable competition.

Handbills advertising the Games will carry banner messages promoting climate action. We have several possibilities under consideration. Our current favourite is: 2028 – IT'S NEVER TOO LATE, which was suggested by Ms Flora McGivern, the vicar's wife. We recognise that marketing is not an area of expertise in which we excel and will be happy to take your advice on this aspect of our submission.

The committee will also be pleased to know that LWAOA does not propose to build any new venues for the 2028 Games. Apart from the vast expense, enormous carbon footprint, and dubious beneficial legacy of such constructions, we are confident that the mound of earth at the north end of Lower Wallop Playing Fields is quite sufficient to accommodate the 300 to 400 spectators we expect to attend, in grassy comfort.

Your sincerely,

Major (Retd.) Jack Chamberlain
Hon. Secretary, LWAOA
Rose Cottage
Lower Wallop
Hampshire
U.K.

Many words for snow

Anna Jonsson

Snow. Snö. There are so many kinds of it; blötsnö (watery snow), pudersnö (powder snow), tö (thaw), nysnö (new snow), skare (frozen crust on the snow), slask (slush)... And dagsmeja. The most beautiful of them all. Snow melting during the day at the return of the sun in springtime, and then freezing again at night. They say that the Sámi language holds more than two hundred words for snow.

I was asked to write a tale about snow and sports, but I am sorry to disappoint you. There will not be a lot of sport in this tale. Snow to me is not sport, it is life. Snow makes the whole difference between light and darkness, between creativity and apathy. Hope and despair.

Living in the Northern hemisphere with dark and long winters, the snow is an essential part of life. Or was. When I grew up in the 1980s and 1990s the winters were always filled with snow. Lots of it. Always there. Surrounding you. Evident and trustworthy. We built caves of snow, we made snowmen and snow lanterns. And we went sledding.

In the schoolyard there was a slope where we went sledding on slippery ice tracks, squiggling between the trees. Until the day a girl broke her arm... As teenagers my friends and I went to the steepest hill in the forest, we went downhill with our snow racers, they went fast... You had to watch out for the trees. Then up and down again. But the best hill of them all, it was by my grandmother's house in Ångermanland, in the middle of Sweden (most Swedes would consider it as north though). It was not really a hill, more like a mountain.

My grandmother's house was an old, big wooden house by a lake. The house used to be the store of the village, and in the store house there were still horseshoes hanging to be sold. And there was this magnificent giant wooden snow sleigh. We pulled it all the way up the mountain with steam billowing from our breaths and the sounds of creaking from our steps in the cold snow. Our bodies were heating up from the effort of climbing all the way up the hill. And then, the big joy of going downhill at such a speed.

But the speed was even faster when me and my father went all the way up with the big kick-sled, I was screaming with delight and fear, and my eyes were filled with tears from the cold air. When I write these words my eyes fill again with tears, but for another reason. Will my grandchildren be able to experience all this?

In Ångermanland there is still snow in the winter. But where I live, more south, in Stockholm it is different. The snow isn't reliable any longer. You never know when, or if, it will come, how much will fall, or how long it will stay. One winter, not long ago, we had a little bit of snow in November, and then just a few days in March. In between there was no snow at all. Not even enough cold to make ice on the lakes.

Can you imagine the darkness without snow? For me, it is hard. The darkness becomes like a wall. And you know, it is not only during the night, in the middle of the winter it is from three in the afternoon until nine the next morning. Even during daytime everything becomes grey and dull. There are no colours. No brightness. Just nuances of brown and grey. You just don't want to go out. Also, because there is nothing to do. No skating. No skiing. No sleigh riding. All you can do is to wait for spring and summer. Winter becomes like a dark tunnel; you must get through it to see the light on the other side.

Snow makes the whole difference. It gives light and opens doors. Gives a magic touch to the world. The sun reflects on the snow, giving you a boost of light better than any other... And the moon reflects too. I remember skiing with friends in the moonlight at Vindelfjällen, in the very north of Sweden. The soft snow surrounding us and weighing down the spruces, transforming them into fantasy creatures in the bleak moonlight.

That day we had been following the footprints of a wolverine all day. Another time we followed the traces of a lynx and her kittens. They had been playing on the ice. We could see their movements. Big cats playing. This was in the national park of Tresticklan, just at the border with Norway. That winter really was a cold one. At the lake nearby there were remarkable patterns in the ice. Each one more astonishing than the other.

Will snow and ice be reminiscent of another time? It feels like I am carrying a treasure, unsure if I will be able to hand it over, the snow thieves ready to take it all.

This is not primarily about my own memories and experiences, but all the generations before mine, struggling in the cold and adapting life to snow and ice. There are also the stories of my parents and grandparents. My grandmother, born in the beginning of the 20th century, told me about the yearly race to the "julotta" (the early service on Christmas day) with horse sleigh – they went fast, very fast... And she was terrified. That must have been about a hundred years ago. What about a hundred years from now on, will there even be any snow at all?

And at the time before the fridge and the freezer, my grandfather used to cut big ice blocks from the lake and cover them with sawdust, in this way they could keep the cold until summer and even make their own ice cream. To my father's delight. He, in his turn, went skiing to school duing wintertime, several kilometres through the forest. When I tell my kids they get terrified. Skiing alone in the dark woods when he was seven years old?! They hardly ever want to go cross country skiing with me, they prefer going downhill. Much faster, much easier.

Now, living in Stockholm in the 2020s we still have some snow – usually for short periods at least each winter. There are even some winters with longer periods of snow. But nowadays the really cold days are very rare, almost gone. The coldness is weak and capricious.

But when those periods come, I become happy like a child. As everyone else, throwing ourselves outdoors – the forest just nearby is filled with people walking, skating, skiing… Smiling. Kids playing and building creatures in the snow. And when the snow disappears. Empty again. No life. People hiding in their houses, hibernating like the badger. There is just a lonesome runner somewhere in the grey forest, having a marathon in summer to think about.

The Long Road:
climate change and
indigenous culture in
professional cycling

Matt Rendell

Prodigious hailstones pummeled the hard earth. Lightning flashes turned night to day and, between the storms, the summer heat was so intense, the very sky seemed made of fire. Eighty of France's ninety-six mainland departments were on severe weather watch the day the 2019 Tour de France entered the Alps. The next, mudslides trapped a hundred travellers between their flows, 35 kilometres beyond the stage finish at Valloire, while, elsewhere in France, 6,500 hectares of farmland and forests burned thanks to heat and drought.

It was a summer of extremes.

Yet, at Saint-Jean-de-Maurienne, for the start of stage nineteen, blue skies welcomed the riders. Only on the Col de l'Iseran did the shadows lose their sharpness, although, with 42.5 kilometres still to ride, Egan Bernal had other things on his mind. There was no change of body shape in his attack. Over the next four kilometres, he overtook the best riders from the early breakaway. Some matched his pace for a moment. All eventually dropped away. He crossed the col alone, two minutes and seven seconds before the previous race leader, Julian Alaphilippe – although, with 15 downhill kilometres before the final 7.4 km climb up to the finish line at Tignes, the day could still hold plenty of racing.

However, while the riders were climbing the Iseran, the weather had moved in at the foot of the descent. In fifteen torrential minutes, dark clouds had deposited six inches of hail, snow and slush on the race route. Quick response snow ploughs bulldozed floodwater from the road, only for more to close in behind them. Worse, 13.5 km from the finish line, beyond the Daille tunnel, a landslide had buried the road in half a metre of debris.

There could be no final ascent, no stage finish at Tignes. The leaders were stopped 800m from the mudslide. The stage was stopped, the riders informed, and the time gaps at the Col d'Iseran confirmed what everyone knew: Egan Bernal was in the yellow jersey.

The following day, after three further mudslides had taken place on the descent of the Cormet de Roselend, and an orange alert issued for thunderstorms, Tour director Christian Prudhomme shortened the stage.

Two days later, on the Champs Elysées, he celebrated Colombia and the developing world's first Tour de France win. It was the strangest of Tours, and one that seemed to mark, not just a freak weather front but a long-term change of climate. On Wednesday 24 July, ozone pollution peaked in the Paris region. The body responsible for monitoring air quality worried that, with global warming, "summer ozone could pose a serious threat to human health, agriculture and natural ecosystems". On Thursday 25 July temperatures over 43°C were recorded across much of the country. Paris broke a 70-year-old record with 42.6°C, leaving shoppers wilting on the Champs-Élysées.

If sport is one of the emblems of modernity, so too is weather made more extreme by human-made climate change. Ironically, the new reality for outdoor sports coincided with the emergence of a generation of cyclists whose forebears contributed little to global emissions, being indigenous people.

To a flicker of sheet lightning, the tropical night engulfs the mountains of Iguaque, which rise like a great wave over Vereda La Concepción, a vereda being a unit of farmland divided among a number of households. The night is cold here in the high altitude Colombian department of Boyacá and, at ten thousand feet above sea level, you sigh involuntarily after each movement.

The darkness above us hides the lake from which, according to the narrative cycles of the Muysca people, Bachué, the primordial woman, emerged in the time of the ancestors to populate the earth. Lower down lie the hillsides where, in what we can only call March 1537 – the other calendar involved being lost – a bearded wayfarer named Gonzalo Jiménez de Quesada appeared at the head of 170 half-starved Spaniards.

The aspiring Conquistadors and their horses had left the Caribbean coast eleven months earlier. Six hundred of their men succumbed en route to exhaustion and disease, before the peaceable Muysca offered them their wary assistance. But the expedition was just one of eight that would subdue these highlands before 1550. Today, the only remaining traces of their culture apparent to the casual observer today are the place names. Vereda La Concepción lies on a hillside about six kilometres from the village of Cómbita, thought to mean either 'Hand of the Tiger' or 'Strength of the Summit.'

I asked Colombian rider, Nairo Quintana, about them: Bachué, the primal mother, Bochica, the lawmaker, Chía, the moon-goddess. What did the old ancestral stories mean today?

He told me, 'That is who we are.'

Yet, as the centuries pass, we understand less and less of the Muysca. Of their language, the last native speaker is believed to have died in around 1870, and most of what remains of it is contained in two documents dispatched from the New World at the end of the eighteenth century for inclusion in

Catherine the Great's Comparative Dictionaries of All Languages and Dialects. When he received them, Charles III, who had ordered the eradication of the indigenous languages in his dominions, decided not to send them on to Saint Petersburg but to keep them in his Chamber Library – which is to say, the idioms described in those priceless parchments were made extinct by their collector. Rarely has the theory that the act of observing alters the thing observed been more heartlessly demonstrated.

Anyway, it could be that the colonial rulers simply corralled a dozen distinct groups into camps and pressed together an array of complex dialects into an elementary Muyscaranto. If so, what we thought we knew of their language, we didn't – and the Conquest did not so much destroy the Muysca people as create them.

The front door opens onto an empty conservatory and then the house proper. Emiro López, in his early sixties, stands on the threshold between the kitchen and the room where his wife, Isabel Monroy, known as Mamá Chavita (Chavita simply means 'small', although she is not especially slight) has for many years run the Pato Lucas Kindergarten. Emiro's eyes glisten as he travels a quarter of a century back in time.

'He was crawling slowly across the floor just here,' he says. 'I picked him up' – he mimes picking up a tiny child and encountering a gaze devoid of all recognition – 'and said to Isabel, "There is no life in him. The boy is going to die."'

Nairito – 'Little Nairo' – eight months old, was emaciated and weak with diarrhoea. His stomach was shockingly swollen, his hair on end. Few believed he would survive infancy.

Standing opposite Emiro, her back to the stove, is Mamá Chavita herself. She tells me, in beautiful, peasant Spanish, 'Tentaron de ese tiempo que lo había tentado era antes de defunto', which I take to mean something like, 'Around that time, he was tempted by a dead body,' the verb tentar having shades of 'to goad,' 'to try the mettle of.' In other words, Nairo had been somehow courted or put to the test by a strange force of attraction emanating from the dead woman.

He had come into the world on 4 February 1990, the son of Luís Quintana, a market trader from neighbouring Vereda Salvial, and his wife Eloísa Rojas. Luís is ruddy, light-skinned, green-eyed. Eloísa has soft, dark, Muysca features. Their faces tell the history of these hills. As a young man, Luís had rented a shack beside a busy road and started selling groceries. It is easy to find: open any online map and search for Tienda la Villita. The imposing house you find now is proof of Luís's acumen: the store allowed him to buy the land – some of which he turned to agriculture – extend the property and marry Eloísa Rojas, a customer from Vereda San Rafael across the road.

Eloísa had been abandoned as a child. She told me, 'I was one of eight children, although I found out only recently. I was brought up by a woman named

Sagrario Rojas, who loved me like her own daughter.'

A few months after Nairo's birth, Sagrario Rojas died. Eloísa had taken the baby with her to pay her respects.

'The illness began three days later,' Eloísa told me. 'The man who had dressed the corpse must have touched little Nairo.'

'Los antiguos,' Isabel Monroy says, meaning the old people of the community, 'told Doña Eloísa' – Nairo's mother – 'to collect the buds of nine medicinal plants, boil them, and bathe Nairito in the water,' and it is unclear from her description whether the ritual act of collecting the buds was not itself part of the cure.

Later, Nairo spoke to me of a belief system going back many years, according to which dead bodies emit a cold energy that, on contact, impregnates unborn children or babes in arms.

'Only natural remedies can be used to treat it. It's not a matter of scientific medicine.' As an athlete, Nairo has been subjected to scientific method since his teens, and knows exactly what he is saying: that modern science and medicine, for all the good they do in the world, belong to a way of life that has forced the thought-world of his own childhood into retreat, which makes Nairo's illness and survival, more than medical or biographical facts, markers of identity, even forms of resistance.

Consider death. A taboo subject in modern culture, but not in Ecuador, where, on the día de los difuntos, peasant farmers flock to the cemeteries with food and flowers. So when, seventeen days after the day of the dead, Richard Carapaz, the 2019 Giro d'Italia champion, suggests we drive the 24 kilometres from his home to the cemetery in Tulcán, the capital of Carchi province, it is entirely normal.

Richard walks us to a section dedicated to the cosmology of the Pasto people, indigenous to the region, then steers the conversation to local Carchi surnames. 'Cuasquer, Cuasapud, Cuasapas, Carapaz... I have friends with all those names. Cuasquer means "Great Chieftain." Carapaz means "the strength of the wind" or "strong like the wind."'

Nothing to do with peace or carapaces, then: through his father, Antonio, Richard is a descendant of the Pastos, which makes him, like Nairo and Dayer Quintana, Darwin Atapuma, Winner Anacona, and a few others, a member of that handful of indigenous riders – post-indigenous, we might say, their language and traditions largely extinguished by the Spanish invaders, and then by Colombian national culture – who have helped shape world cycling over the past decade. Richard stops over a tombstone and looks down.

Juan Carlos Rosero García. Ecuador's most successful cyclist (until his pupil, Richard Carapaz). Three Vueltas a Ecuador, the leader's jersey from start to finish in 1992, the only foreign winner, that same year, his annus mirabilis, of the hard-fought Vuelta a Boyacá in Colombia, and fifth in the Vuelta a Colombia, displacing Lucho Herrera from the race lead for a day.

Briefly a Pepsi Cola-Alba-Fanini rider in Italy, where he was listed as Colombian. And later, much later, the man who made a cyclist of Richard Carapaz, who calls him, 'My friend, my brother, my second father.'

Born 28 November 1962. Died 23 January 2013, a day Richard will never forget.

That morning, Juan Carlos Rosero, Richard and five or six team-mates set off for a pre-season jog in the mountains.

'We dropped him on the climbs and he caught us on the descents, as usual. Then he began to feel ill and decided to turn back. When we finished, I called him to see if he could pick us up. At first he said no. Then he called back and said, "I'm on my way." He met us, dropped us off, and then, three hours later, the phone rang. I thought there had been some sort of mix up. Or it was a bad joke. I ran to the emergency room, but they sent me to the morgue, where I found his family weeping.

'It was the first time I had lost a loved one.'

And that was how the four days of our visit went: Richard, tactfully and expertly revealing selected regions of his soul, structuring a story I only had to write. If winning a Grand Tour is itself a supreme act of storytelling, Richard's skill in the art extends to the presentation of himself to the world.

Elsewhere in the cemetery, he stops beside another grave: José María Carapaz, died 16 August 2019. Richard's paternal grandfather, an Ecuadorean married to a Colombian, hunter, charcoal burner and cross-border trader, working the exchange rates to turn a profit. Standard practice here: the shops accept Colombian pesos and the US dollar, Ecuadorean currency since the Sucre was phased out in 2000 – and small coins barely used in the USA get a new life here, anything larger than a $20 bill being hard to change. Ecuadoreans cross into Colombia to buy electrical goods, Colombians cross into Ecuador to buy fuel and clothes, the money-changers at the crossing give better rates than the banks. and smuggling of every type is rife. Cars with concealed tanks spirit subsidised Ecuadorean petrol past the guards.

This border culture breeds street sharpness, and a sense of difference from the rest of the country. The land is fertile, and Richard tells me, 'Carchi supplies Ecuador with potatoes, sweetcorn, spring onions – and cyclists. When I won the Giro, the people wanted the victory for themselves, and made jokes about the independent republic of Carchi.'

His grandfather, José María, made enough to buy out his brothers and sisters and unify the family land. Gravely ill throughout Richard's triumphant Giro, he died on 16 August 2019, the day Richard salvaged a podium place in the Tour of Burgos after his team leader Antonio Pedrero's form collapsed.

The following morning, we follow in Richard's car as he rides between the farmsteads where he grew up. The gradients are steep here, the altitude close to 3200 metres, yet Richard doesn't sweat or even seem to breath.

'Juan Carlos used to tell me, "This isn't altitude training. We are adapted to living here. We have the right physique."'

There is no beach at La Playa: before the River Chingual was diverted to irrigate intensive agriculture (Richard tells me, 'All the government cares about is productivity. The peasant farmers are abandoned to their fate'), silt accumulated into sandy banks and gave the area its name. A keen fisherman, Richard often used to catch breakfast with a pole and line. Today only a creek remains, crossing a triangle of land with a volcano at each corner – Cumbal and Chiles on the Colombian side to the north, Reventador to the south – and La Playa at its centre. Richard's family has lived here for four generations, since one of his great-grandfathers, a soldier, came here from San Gabriel, 14 kilometres and a world away.

They were small farmers, Richard says, 'until my father switched to driving a truck. For fifteen years he transported coffee from the Ecuadorian Amazon, through the border controls, to the coffee warehouses at Ipiales in Colombia.'

The white, five-roomed house Richard grew up in stands atop a steep drive, opposite the crater of an extinct volcano. In the mornings, hummingbirds visit the ranks of potted orchids beside the door, some of them presents from her attentive son. A keen catcher of the gigantic trout that abound in the local rivers, Richard points out trees and fruit perhaps unknown to his foreign visitors: chinguacán, related to papaya;

mortiño, similar to blueberry; taxo, called curuba in Colombia, a sort of passion fruit native to the cloud forest; ovo, native to the area around Ibarra.

In 1991, after ten childless years, Antonio Carapaz and Ana Luísa Montenegro resolved to travel to the capital for fertility tests. First they needed the proceeds from the next potato crop. But before it sprouted, Ana Luísa, aged 40, discovered, to their joy, that she was pregnant. A daughter, Marcela, arrived in 1992. Richard came a year later, on 29 May 1993, and then, the next year, Cristina. When Richard was still small, his parents made the annual 6 September pilgrimage over the border to the remarkable Las Lajas Sanctuary in the canyon of the Guáitara River, to give thanks for the blessing of children.

After primary school at La Playa, Richard, aged 11, went to the secondary school at El Playón de San Francisco, on the dividing line between the border provinces of Carchi and Sucumbíos, 4 kilometres away as the crow flies, 9 kilometres along the unmade road. At first an old 4x4 served as a school bus, making several trips to pick up all the La Playa kids. Then, aged fourteen, he found a bike in a shipment of junk his father had picked up.

'My old bike was broken, so I climbed into the truck and found another one in perfect condition. I wore the tires down to nothing, then rode on the rims.'

Good enough in his studies to be made an escolta, a kind of prefect, he was an inter-school athlete until he discovered cycling. It nearly never happened. Late in 2007, the owner of a national road-construction firm called Panavial, supported by the Prefecture of Carchi, encouraged Juan Carlos Rosero to pass on his experience to a new generation of riders. The day Rosero visited El Playón de San Francisco and invited the pupils to join his newly constituted cycling club, it was a time of family crisis and Richard was absent. His mother, Ana Luisa – Anita – had been diagnosed with breast cancer. Antonio was moving mountains to ensure she got the necessary treatment, leaving Richard and his grandfather in charge of the smallholding. Their eight cows needed milking by hand, and the 120 litres carrying down to the roadside, and they had been difficult that morning. Richard did not finish milking until 9am, and school finished at 12.30, so it was hardly worth going.

The next day, his schoolmate Amilcar Pozo told him about Rosero's visit. Richard went to see him and joined the 50 or 60 other students who had enrolled. Work started in January 2008 with physical conditioning, and the first pupils dropped out. Then, on the track at Tulcán, the first crashes thinned them out further.

Richard's other schoolmates are farmers, teachers, housewives, security guards. Some might conclude that life in Carchi has little to offer. Richard disagrees: it offers birdsong, he says, and double rainbows, and fertile fields, and human solidarity.

'Every time you go out, you have to take your rain cape. There are supposed to be two satellites monitoring the weather, but the only reliable forecast is when a peasant farmer looks up at the sky.'

The mountains above La Playa are covered with the dense virgin forests of the Guandera Biological Reserve, teeming with deer, tapir, spectacled bear and large rodents called mountain paca. The hillsides boil with natural springs.

'Until I was ten, I had no idea there was an outside world. My mother would say, "Go and see how the birds sing" or "Go and count the butterflies," and I did. I feel I come from another world. There are things I can't explain to my team-mates. You have to come here to understand.'

That said, he recalls, 'When I was a child, there were FARC attacks and car bombs the other side of the border. They closed the crossing from time to time, but it always opened again.'

The Colombian border is only two or three kilometres away. With no road on the Colombian side, the illegal armed groups used this one. And the Reserve is only semi-explored, even today.

'It's the sort of terrain the guerrillas like to hide in,' Richard says.

In the 1990s and 2000s, Antonio Carapaz was held up twice by Colombian armed groups. He still remembers the ants crawling on his skin as he lay on the ground, his hands zip tied behind his back.

Richard has lived in the small town of Julio Andrade, 20 kilometres from Tulcán (and named after a nineteenth-century general) since 2013 when his team at the time, RPM-Ecuador, insisted its riders move there.

'I thought I would be spending the rest of my career there, so I bought land and built a house.'

At Zacatecas, Mexico in May 2013, at the Pan-American Championships under-23 road road race, his horizons shifted again.

'Before his death, Juan Carlos had fixed that race as my season's goal. He said, "It will open the door, Richard finished the race one minute and fifty-two seconds ahead of the runner-up. Two months later he was competing in Europe with the Ecuadorian national team, riding the four-day Tour des Pays de Savoie in France, an 18 year old among elite riders. He finished the first three stages fourth, fifth and second, and ninth overall.

In January 2015 he joined the Medellín-based team Strongman–Campagnolo. That April he won stage three of the 2015 Vuelta de la Juventud – the under-23 version of the Vuelta a Colombia – and pulled on the leader's jersey. Twenty-four hours later, he won atop the 22 kilometre climb to Concordia. Tulcán received the race's first ever non-Colombian champion with a five-hour parade.

It was a mere waypoint in a meteoric ascent. He started 2016 in Colombia riding for Strongman-Campagnolo Wilier.

There too he thought he would ride out his career, until Juanjo Oróz, the ex-Euskadi rider, now the director of Lizarte, effectively, Movistar's development team in Pamplona, Spain, called. Richard travelled to Europe and, over an eight week period spanning March, April and May 2016, took four wins, four second places, and a third, all the while gifting wins to teammates, making friends and allies, earning widespread admiration. In August 2016 he became the first ever Ecuadorean on a WorldTour team. At the 2018 Giro he won Ecuador's first grand tour stage. In 2019, he took his country's first grand tour win.

Ecuador lies very much in the margins of the world sports system. So unfamiliar are Ecuadoreans with winning that, on the final stage of his victorious Giro d'Italia, when it was nigh impossible for Richard to lose, the locals were betting against him.

Richard explains, 'They thought it was impossible for an Ecuadorian to win. That is Ecuador: we have a culture of losing, of being unable to take decisions. When I was wearing the Maglia Rosa, everyone still thought I would crash, or something would happen.'

After Richard's Giro d'Italia win in 2019, Ecuador was hit by violent demonstrations after President Lenin Moreno decided to bow to the demands of the International Monetary Fund by cutting fuel subsidies. It was a precondition for loans totalling US$4.2 billion.

'Three quarters of Ecuadoreans are poor,' Richard explains. 'Of them, a third live in extreme poverty. If fuel goes up, everything goes up. The minimum wage is only US$380 a month, so if you cut the fuel subsidy, you have to raise the minimum wage.'

As a result, Richard had given his support, not to the violence, but to the cause of the rural poor. Like his insistence of his indigenous identity, it was an early sign of intent to bring his success in international sport to bear on local realities – to deploy globalisation against its own uniformalising tendencies.

The outside world reached this corner of the earth half a millennium ago. As our bus descended into the sweltering, sugar-growing regions, we see its traces: Afro-descendant settlements whose inhabitants speak Palenquero, a fascinating and unique creole developed among those who escaped their bonds and gathered in fortified refuges called palenques, where their African languages mixed with the Spanish and Portuguese of their enslavers.

Richard says, 'I love the way they speak: it is very sweet.'

I am interested to know how different he feels from his European team-mates, the Venn diagram of his soul being so crowded with overlapping circles, all of them – Ecuadorean, campesino, Amerindian – atypical in the WorldTour.

'And Afro-descendant,' he volunteers.

'Sorry?'

'Through my mother. Her father is black. Her brothers and sisters are dark-skinned.'

And I felt how his rivals must have felt during the 2019 Giro: every time you think you have captured Richard Carapaz, he escapes you.

We carry our past and our childhood with us. For the EF Education First – Nippo rider Neilson Powless, the winner of the Clásica San Sebastián on 31 July 2021, they include a chilling tale of racial violence and revenge he heard many times growing up.

Simon Antoine, an Oneida Native American, was jumped by four white men. They beat him to a pulp, gouged out one of his eyes and left him for dead. But Simon Antoine survived. He crawled to safety, regained his strength, then hunted down his assailants and killed them one by one.

When this took place before or after the 1820s, when the Oneida were removed from what white America calls New York State to Wisconsin, a thousand miles away, is unclear. But Simon Antoine certainly existed. He lived into the age of photography and posed for a picture that made its way down the generations to Neilson's father Jack Powless. When Neilson and his older sister Shayna, also a professional cyclist, were growing up, the photo hung on the wall of their parents' room at home in Roseville, California, 20 miles northeast of Sacramento in northern California.

They speak of Simon Antoine with pride. Jack even had his ancestor's image depicted in gold leaf on the bodywork of his Harley Davidson.

Perhaps, as Neilson mustered the speed to pass the formidable Matej Mohorič in the final sprint at San Sebastián, the memory of Simon Antoine helped.

'I guess,' he says, 'maybe subconsciously you kind of think, "We've got the same blood in us."'

Neilson Powless was a prodigy. Fourth in the US national time trial championships for 17 and 18 year olds when he was 15, he won the amateur division in the World XTERRA off-road triathlon championships in Hawaii, aged 16, the youngest ever winner. On his way to victory there, he whipped 17 professional triathletes and the winners of all the older amateur age groups.

As a mountain biker, he won the junior US short track cross-country title in 2014. The same year, at the Continental Championships in Brazil, he finished fourth behind the Mexican winner, José Gerardo Ulloa, and the two Colombians Brandon Rivera and Egan Bernal. Weeks later, in a warm-up race for the 2014 Junior World Championships at Hafjell, Norway, he finished third, one second and one place ahead of Bernal. In Norway, Bernal took the silver medal. Powless, the day after his 18th birthday, finished eighth.

In 2017, five days after finishing second in the elite US road championships, he won the under-23 national title. His talent attracted international attention and, the following year, he joined Team Jumbo Visma and moved abroad for the first time. Signed for two years, Powless describes his stint with the Dutch team as 'a critical growing experience. I had some decent races but overall I felt I was underperforming.'

In 2020 he moved to EF Education First, in his words, 'coming back into a space I was really comfortable with.' The 2021 Clásica San Sebastián was his first WorldTour win. Even so, EF boss Jonathan Vaughters described him as 'the next phase in the team's stage racing ambitions.'

Yet Powless never planned a career in cycling. Left to his own devices, he might have followed his grandfather, Jack's father Matt Powless, into boxing. Matt grew up in Tigerton, Wisconsin, between the Stockbridge–Munsee and Menomenee Indian Reservations, and the Oneida Reservation close to Lake Michigan. In the 1950s, Matt was stationed in Germany with the 82nd Airborne, and became a champion featherweight boxer.

Jack recalls, 'He came out and became a welder and machinist, but he continued to box. Later, he opened a boxing gym on the Stockbridge Reservation. He was very passionate about it. He wanted to give something back.'

Nielson was a natural, with great hand-eye coordination and exceptional speed and power. One summer, after going to the gym on the reservation with his grandfather Matt, Neilson went back to California determined to succeed in the ring.

He told me, 'My parents reluctantly helped me find a boxing gym behind the Roseville Police Station.'

Jack recalled, 'The first day they were circuit training. Neilson just nailed it. The coach said afterwards, "This kid wants to be a boxer, he can go all the way."'

Fortunately, unlike Native Americans of previous generations, Neilson had no pressing need for skill in the art of violence. 'My sister somehow came out looking very dark and much more native than I did. She has my dad's skin colour and I have my mom's. I think, because I look so, you know, white, I never had any issues.'

In any case, as Neilson told me, 'My mom didn't like boxing, and I stopped after a year or so because I was getting pretty busy with endurance athletics.'

From the ages of 8 to 14, he attended a private Christian school where his ethnicity was never an issue. Then he moved to a public high school, mainly in search of competitive athletics.

'I already knew so many people at the school through athletics and cross country and I just got along with most people. In any case, being an athlete in high school makes things a lot easier in America.'

Sport was always part of his childhood. Neilson told me, 'Both my parents were coaches. They were really excited about teaching kids and people growing up and I think a lot of their athlete mindset just kind of bleeds over into their parenting and the way they go about life. They coached the youth triathlon team that my sister and I were on, and sort of kept a really nice group of kids around us that we could all train with and have fun with.'

His father Jack had gone into the Air Force as an aircraft mechanic.

'On my second tour I was assigned to Andersen Air Force Base in Guam. While I was there I started doing triathlons. I wanted to do the Ironman World

Championships, and I qualified in about my second triathlon. I went to Hawaii representing the Air Force and I did pretty good on my first one. I went back in 1992 and got second overall in the military division, and then I won the military division overall in 1993 and 1995.'

Guam was also where Jack Powless met his wife, Los Angeles-born, Sacramento-raised Jen Allred. One of six kids whose father was the assistant coach at the United San Juan club in Sacramento, she was another exceptional athlete. By the time she was seven, Jen held the under-8 world records for the 660 and 880 yards. At 14, she was ranked in the top-10 road racers in the United States. By the time she was 16, she says, 'I was burned out, and determined never to run again.'

Three years later, she walked into American River College mid-season and asked to join the cross-country squad. Attracted by the sports scholarship which would mean she would not have to work while attending college, she says, 'I was completely out of shape, and came in dead last in my first race. But the next year I came out state champion with the nation's fastest time and a scholarship for California State University, Northridge.'

After graduation, while working as a bartender and model, she auditioned for a job as a dancer at the Pacific Islands Club, a Japanese-owned beach resort in Guam. It was 1986. I decided to give it six months and I ended up loving it. I got into diving, started running again, and, working with Japanese clients, I

78

learned the language and became a flight attendant, which allowed me to race all over the Pacific.'

Guam's National Olympic Committee, founded in 1976, was recognised by the International Olympic Committee in 1986, giving the island a new sporting independence. Jen achieved the qualifying time to run the Olympic marathon at Seoul in 1988, but confusion over residency requirements prevented her from racing. She ran the marathon for Guam at the 1992 Games in Barcelona, finishing 36th in 3:14.45, with no coaching or training facilities. Two weeks later, Guam's number one male and female triathletes married.

Elected Air Force Athlete of the Year 1992, Jack was transferred to Special Operations Command in Hurlburt Field, Florida, and ran the Commando fitness program for the next seven years. Their daughter Shayna was born in Florida in January 1994. Jen qualified for the Atlanta Olympics in 1996 but did not run. Instead, eight months pregnant with her second child, Neilson, she worked as a volunteer at the Game. She described him as 'my Olympian baby.' Within a week of the birth, Jen took him to the YMCA swimming pool.

When Jack was transferred to Beale Air Force Base in Northern California, in his original role as an aircraft mechanic, working on U-2s, Jen started coaching the women's track and field and cross country teams at American River College in Sacramento, a post she still holds. Jack retired from the Air Force in 2001, his hearing damaged by years of working close to jet engines.

He described their approach to parenting. 'Jen made sure they got a taste of everything. We tried to keep everything fun and we never really pushed them. The one rule was, whatever sport they chose, they had see get through the end of that season because other people depended on them.'

Neilson ran cross country for his high school, finishing 8th in the State Championships and setting a record for the Mount Sac course in Los Angeles. He won the 11-12 age group at the 2008 USA Triathlon Youth and Junior National Championships. In 2011 he became the US off-road triathlon champion in the 15-19 age group. In 2012, aged 16, Neilson won the US and world championship overall titles in the 15-19 age group, and became the youngest ever overall winner in the amateur division in both races. He repeated the feat at the world championships in Kapalua, Maui. In 2010 Shayna, 16, dominated the 15-19 age group at the US off-road triathlon championship, then, in 2013, became the national under-23 cross country mountain bike champion.

Neilson began to combine mountain biking on the US national team with road-racing. Soon, Neilson learned that he was not the first Oneida road racer. The son of an Oneida mother and a half-Indian, half-Belgian father, Cole House was born in 1988 and raised on the Oneida Reservation in Wisconsin. Helped by a scheme to promote sport and fitness through mountain bike racing between Oneida, Blackfoot and other Native American youngsters, he won a stage at the prestigious Tour de l'Abitibi in Québec, and moved to Flanders with the U.S. national team. Seventh at the 2008 under-23 Tour of Flanders, he rode on BMC's under-23 development team in 2009, and won the GP Waregem, outsprinting Jens Debusschere and Jens Keukeleire. In 2011, as a stagiaire for BMC's ProTour team, he was ninth in the Kampioenschap van Vlaanderen, just behind his roommate Alexander Kristoff, and Radioshack's Gert Steegmans. Even so, after failing to finish nine of the 15 races he started for BMC, Cole returned home with his chances of a pro career in tatters.

For the 2015 season, Neilson, a first-year under-23 rider, spent half the year riding in the US with Hagens Berman, and the other half in Europe with the national team. In 2016 Hagens Berman merged with Axel Merckx's development team Axeon.

Neilson recalled, 'I think I was actually the only rider they brought over.'

In 2016, his sister Shayna graduated with a B.A. in Psychology from the University of California, Los Angeles (UCLA). She had won her place there in 2012, although her parents' limited income made taking it up unlikely, until the Oneida nation stepped in. One of the more organised Native American nations, the Oneida had invested wisely the profits from a controversial sector. Gaming in massive casinos built on fiscally independent indigenous reservations has been common since the 1970s. The US Congress legalised the industry through the 1988

Indian Gaming Regulatory Act, securing a cut of the profits for white America. The activist Thomas King, in his book 'The Inconvenient Indian,' observes that 'industrial-strength gambling contributes little of value to the world [and] generally brings out the worst in folks, Native as well as non-Native,' yet the Oneida have used their earnings to buy back lost land in New York State and Wisconsin, fund reservation infrastructure, and provide social services for the aged and education for the young. Neilson would have qualified for similar support, had the matter of college ever come up.

But 2016 was the year the big WorldTour teams began to take notice of him. After winning the Joe Martin Stage Race overall, as well as the points and best young rider competitions, and finishing third in the Tour of the Gila time trial on his way to 12th overall, he went to the Amgen Tour of California with Axeon Hagens Berman, and finished fifth in stage three, ending on a seven kilometre final climb. He was sixth the following day, and ninth overall. Three months later, helping his teammate Adrien Costa make the podium of the Tour de l'Avenir, while finishing second to Costa in the individual time trial, and defeating Egan Bernal and David Gaudu, among others, on the queen stage over La Toussuire to the Col de la Croix de Fer.

His current success is built on deep foundations.

Yet what sets Shayna, a professional with Team TWENTY24, and Neilson apart is their determination to use their sporting careers to improve the lives of other Native Americans. Shayna and her partner, the American footballer Eli Ankou (an Ojibwe of the Dokis First Nation through his mother) back a non-profit organisation called the Dreamcatcher Foundation, empowering youth through sports, and bringing awareness to the issue of missing and murdered indigenous women and girls in North America.

Shayna told me, 'Most Oneida kids have good access to resources and funding, but most reservations are in secluded rural areas, where the young have very limited opportunities. Those are the areas we target.'

And there is a quiet Oneida dimension to the rites of passage that punctuate the Powless's lives. Neilson's childhood interest in ballet was rekindled in November 2019 when he met Frances Chae of the Sacramento Ballet. They married a year later. After the wedding, Jack followed the wedding Oneida tradition by spreading tobacco on the ground where they were married to thank the Earth.

When they can find the time, Shayna and Neilson plan to return to the reservation for the ritual by which the tribe confers on them their Oneida names. Jack's is Tea-Ho-Huyea-Tasea, meaning 'Who Has Travelled Far.' His children look destined to travel further still.

From Jim Thorpe at the 1912 Olympics to Cathy Freeman in 2000, from Kenya's Kalenjin distance runners to Chile's many Mapuche footballers, Shayna and Neilson, indigenous people have always been in sport. Western modernity uses it as a mechanism of assimilation, paying indigenous athletes, sometimes very handsomely, to become actors in our culture of exhibitionism. In this way, it tries to buy them out. They resist, and turn the culture of sporting celebrity against itself, by strengthening the values and identity of their communities. In this way, as modernity's race towards ecological destruction accelerates, it undermines itself, and creates a pole of resistance we should support.

Crossing paths

Deborah Rim Moiso

I – Waking up

A bear waking up

Feeling the muscles twitching inside my back, and hunger. Turning around in my warm space. Yawning. Snapping my jaw. Scratching against the sandy soil. Tingling in my legs and paws and a will to stand. Smell of fresh snow in the air, cold and crisp. Dilated nostrils. Turning around. Standing up. Walking out. Shaking my fur. Getting used to the light. Bright, bright, white light. Shaking again. Smelling snow. Smelling fox. Crouching in snow. Turning in snow. Rolling! Sliding! Shaking. Running in snow! White, cold, wet. A drive arises— in that direction: rosehip bushes, sweet after frost. Walking in the snow now.

A human waking up

Finally a weekend with some sunshine. I've been monitoring the weather report constantly, hoping for sunshine, and snow, so I can go up to the mountains on snowshoes. I thought I'd be using them every weekend along the wood trails next to my house, throughout the winter months. Wishful thinking. The blizzards that forced my ancestors to the house for days are ancient history. Nowadays, snow comes to the Apennine foothills in timid flurries that barely cover the rooftops. The changing patterns are so evident, so one-year-to-the-next, that I no longer have to worry as I used to about freezing faucets and broken pipes.

Snowshoes are such fun. The first outing of the year is harsh on the ankles, but it's a good feeling, the effort in muscles that had so far been hibernating, unused parts of the body coming to life. New tracks to be made where it would otherwise be implausible to tread. Everywhere is possible, with snowshoes!

I walk from room to room picking out items for the outing, placing each object on the kitchen table before packing them all up.

Gloves, a wool hat. Extra socks to change in case mine get wet. Water bottles. Two boiled eggs. Bread. Cheese. Chocolate. I make my own trail mix— mixing hazelnuts, shelled almonds, Turkish sultanas, cranberries and dried coconut cubes. I mix it all up nicely in resealable plastic bags.

II – On the way

A bear on the way

Walking. Snow under my paws. Compacting snow makes a crunch. Listening. The smell of soil is dark and wet and very close. Thin snow. Grass blades peeking through. Eating grass is green and munchy. Cold and wet. A memory of rosehip, red sweet tart. Over the hill then. Walking in the snow.

A human on the way

It takes about an hour driving along a slow road of curves and potholes before getting to the mountain proper. The road sticks close to a cold stream. The riverbed is full of water now, swift and gray. We had so little snow this year and it's already melting, snowmelt all of a sudden, all together, all now, when it's not really useful. And there will be none left later, in high summer, when we need it. I've vaguely heard of a nationwide plan to encourage the building of a vast network of small containment basins for rainwater, and of the low likelihood of it ever actually getting implemented.

III – Considering others

A bear considering others

*Walking. A smell envelops this tree, marked on the
bark, a message from another One, the tree saying
it belongs to the other One. I get on my back feet,
stretch up. Sinews muscles feeling good, strong. I
sink my claws in the bark. Soft bark, sap feeling!
Tree is awake now. Three new claw marks now.
Tree is my tree now. Sap! Smell of green and snow
together! Snow feels wet. Shaking my fur. Walking.*

A human considering others

Up on the mountains, just over the altitude at which
villages are built, I can see some snow cover. I'll park
the car up there, just outside the village walls, where
the paved road ends and muddy tracks begin. These
dirt roads are everywhere up the mountains, suitable
for the many 4x4 vehicles which hunters and farmers
use to drive from pasture to pasture, or to the hidden
huts they keep in so many corners of the woods, to
hunt birds, roe deer, wild boar.

I don't personally know any hunters. I see them
hanging out in groups of three or four, in the villages,
next to their cars. My clothing is not like theirs. They
wear camouflage, I wear bright reds and oranges,
high-visibility polyester hiking gear. I want to make
sure hunters see me and do not take me for a wild
boar, a roe deer, or a bear.

Politically, I am supposed to dislike hunters, look

down on them, be adversarial. In reality, I cannot bring myself to. I guess I envy them, their sure-footedness in the mountains, in the villages too. They 'so belong'.

IV – Being warned

A human being warned

Each small village in these parts has a tiny bar, usually close to the main entrance to the old town. It's not called a bar though, it's a *circolo*. A sign on the door says access for members only, which is not literally true, it's a way to get tax breaks and ensure these places, the places where people meet, can stay open.

This *circolo* contains: a wooden counter, a professional coffee machine, a few dusty shelves of chips, gum and candy, some framed pictures of the village in the old days, black and white or sepia. The man behind the counter is elderly, with bushy eyebrows and shiny brown eyes. I put down my backpack and ask for a coffee.

I don't really want coffee, I want to contribute to the local economy. The old man glances at the snowshoes tied to my backpack. "You're going up the mountain?" His voice is tinged with the soft local accent. "Yes" I nod. "I'll be taking hiking trail number two, up to the fields close to the pass, then around the other side through the pine reforestation projects". I consider it good manners to offer information on my intended routes to anyone I meet while hiking, in case anything happens to me and a search party is sent out.

"The park guide left those, if you want one, they're free." The bartender gestures towards a wicker basket full of small metal chimes. I pick one up – it tinkles. Each bell is hooked to a keychain engraved with the national park's symbol: a Marsican brown bear in profile, looking very much like a teddy.

"Do these work?" He shrugs. "Park staff" he declares, raising an eyebrow in such a way as to imply decades of diffidence between the national authorities and the locals. "They do say so. It's still early for bears to be around, in any case." I nod and smirk in a way that should signify siding with the locals rather than with University types—this is a lie of convenience, as I myself am a University type. Still, I pick up the bell and tie it to my backpack. It's a pretty little thing and can do no harm. I leave a few coins on the counter, and go.

A bear being warned

Walking. Legs warming, muscles warming. Moving to be under the pine trees, away from snow. Wet smells. No food under the pine trees: just pine trees. Broken branches. Soft black soil. Marks are made bright on tree trunks, white red saying these trees are not my trees. These are human trees. Trees in rows, like humans.

Humans make the mountains do things in new ways. The path smells like humans, human path. There are no humans now, not close. Humans make danger, humans attract dogs, humans take up space. This human path is easy to walk inside, but strange. Walking in the mud.

V – Climbing up

A human climbing up

As soon as I am out of the village I turn to face the mountain and begin the climb uphill. As soon as the snow cover is thick enough, I put my snowshoes on the ground and fit them on . There are many marks in the snow, this close to the village—other snowshoes, boots, tracks of a sled being pulled by daddy or mommy up the hill.

A few minutes go by and I am already high above the village and can see the rooftops through gaps in the vegetation: this path starts steep. I stay to the side, enjoying the feeling of having snowshoes on, the buoyancy of a wider surface to walk upon. I keep an eye on the markers painted on the tree trunks to indicate the path, in white and red, the colors of the national hiking organization. Footprints are scarce up herer: marks left by two or three people with Nordic walking poles, which are much in fashion. Bird tracks on the side of the path. Animal tracks crossing the path: a fox perhaps? Or just a cat?

The snowshoes weigh my ankles down. My heart

is pounding. I am short of breath, and sweating. With every step, the bell tied to my backpack tinkles. Is it pleasant or annoying? I haven't decided. Once I tried tying a bell like this to a collar fitted around my cat's neck. I'd read an article about how horrible cats are to local wildlife.

A bell around a cat's neck is supposed to make it impossible for them to be hunters. A bell on my backpack is supposed to make it impossible for me to be prey.

On the 5th of March, 2023, a 26-year old went out for a run and was killed by a brown bear in the region of Trentino, in the Italian Alps. This was the first time such a thing happened in our Country; it caused an uproar. I guess that is why the park is giving away bells now. The bear that killed the runner was eventually captured. A female, with three cubs. Possibly the young fellow startled her. Possibly the bear had not heard his approach. Possibly he ran right between her and her cubs. Possibly she'd had a bad day.

It must be noted that brown bears in the Alps and Marsican bears in the Apennines, a subspecies, are different in size and temperament. The likelihood of a Marsican bear attacking a human is much, much lower. Still, how could I dismiss it as impossible?

I am beginning to appreciate the bell. There are bears up this mountain. This is a known fact. This fact enchants the mountain.

Looking over the vast oak forests on the other side

of a gorge I wonder—is a bear asleep there, under a ledge, inside a cave? Are the wolves on the move? Could a lynx be hiding in the shadows? There are wild boar, roe deer, porcupines, fox and hare and wild goats as well. Chamois, higher up, past the treeline. Yet it is the bear, the wolves, the lynx that make the woods enchanted in my mind. Why is that? Because they could kill me, if they wanted to? And yet they do not want to?

A bear climbing up

The crow caws. The forest goes quiet. I walk in quiet forests. Even the wolf-pack makes way. Smelling their prey, walking to it, seeing them wobble away, eating meat. That was in the last snow. Not in this snoRw. The pack is far away. No wolf-smell, no blood-smell. Walking.

VI – Crossing paths

A bear crossing paths

Higher ground. Heat from the sun, wet ground. Walking exposed, on the ridge. The fields where rosehip grows are closer now. They were there last snow and will be there next snow. Mother's teachings. Traveling the round circle way of Mother. Rosehips, cherries, ants, apples, pears, buckthorn. Honey. Walking. Smell of melted snow. Smell of human things? Smell of human.

Stopping and standing. To see far. Hear far. Feel far. Hearing steps, breathing, and new sounds that scratch the ears. Steering clear is Mother's teachings. Turning away from the path. Moving inside bushes and thickets. Changing ways.

A human crossing paths

I trudge along to the pass. It is gorgeous up here! The view stretched to both sides of the valley. I stop to take it in, take some pictures. It's almost midday now, the sun is beating down hard. It's melting all the snow already. I hear thumping from the woods; it must be the accumulated snow now falling from tree branches.

The path in front of me, leading down through the pine forests, is all muddy now. This slope faces East, the morning sun is stronger on this side. Reluctantly, I take my snowshoes off and tie them back on the pack. I can no longer see tracks. The snow having melted so soon, there is no way to tell if anybody's been here before me, or traveled up the other side.

Poems

Verity Ockenden

These poems were written on my homecoming after two years spent as a collegiate athlete in the small oil town of Beaumont, Texas. Our university campus was situated right next to an Exxon Mobil plant which caught fire occasionally, and oozed sulphurous fumes most of the rest of the time. It was always humid and the leaves of the few trees that stood seemed never to colour or fall; a strangely season-less place. During a period of loss that followed graduation, a return to such green and ancient training routes as the coombes and cattle droves that stretch between Shaftesbury and Salisbury acted as an emotional and physical balm. Their worn yet wild expanses showed me different sides daily, and gave rise to a poem almost every time I unlaced my trainers.

Cornfield Blues

This evening
Earth absorbs
the leaden strike of a soul
on her cut cornfields
shakes a cumulous of clay
from her greying skies
lets the pendulous thud
of a hammering heart
bring damp veins of stolen soil
streaking down her horizon.
This evening
the World takes off her make-up
and gently cloaks my ankles
with the remnants of her day.

Sixteen Miles

Sixteen miles I listen to the alternate slap
of wet plait on scapulae
rain beading oiled thighs like rosaries
cold brow open to the sky
save for the orange strobe of the underpass
as far as two exhalations
will take me
Thaw
Scaled silver, streaked gold
dawn looms and I swim
arctic lengths of a lactic lake
I have created

and only the tides of blood
dashing to shrieking fingertips
tarnish the waters, snag ripples hooklike
into mackerel underbelly
and through it I claw onwards
crab-handed

Wingreen

The true victory lies
at the crown of a frost-gilt hill
where you
pushed feelings like blood
into anguished arteries
where you
let your howling breath be
born away on the wind
where you made war
with the road
and peace with
yourself

Bedsheets

How is it that each morning
the world wakes up
with an air so fresh
while her hills lie crumpled
beneath my feet in beaten folds
like the bedsheets
of a thousand sleepless nights

Needles

Like a broken compass
you race feverishly from your cabin
at the drop of a fir's needle
lightning struck legs, white
as split oak in the moonlight
pining for a north star
while your blood churns
so circularly back to the start

The Snow Thief

Andrew Simms

I remember snow. I cannot forget. My child disappeared in a blizzard.

You might think, then, that I am pleased snow no longer falls. Or, that when a rare flurry dances against my window, it lasts as briefly as a cloud of breath.

But you would be wrong. Somewhere I think my child and the snow may still be together. And, if the snow were to return...

Of course, these are things we cannot know, yet it is something to hold, like the stick picked from the thicket of woods that supports me walking through this overgrown maze of days.

But wait, I am beginning to ramble (in that other way). Let me explain. Let me tell you the story of the snow thieves.

I have – had – three children, by the names of Dawn, Dusk and Midnight. Each had characters to match. You will see. Their favourite winter game was to find the footsteps of the Arctic hare, follow them and hope to be gifted with a ghostly glimpse of its white ears, raised like small sails against the wider sea of whiteness.

Local legend had it that to find the hare in this way would grant your dearest wish for the next year. But, it is possible to wish for something too much. You can probably guess how often, and against my better judgement, I have sought the hare. Not, like the children, out of joyful play, but to see my own child again.

Dawn, my eldest, loved to ski, billowing up clouds of chill diamond dust from the morning's untouched surface hoar. Dusk, my middle child, would skate, swooping and looping on frozen rivers and lakes with the same grace as an Arctic tern. Midnight, my youngest, was different. Midnight would walk and run in the snow, not to pass through the landscape, but to become part of it. When I saw the winter sun on her face – *apricity* they call this peculiar warmth – wrapped up to follow the hare's footsteps, it was as if she was already gone, communing with another.

Events began ten years before, at the Frost Fayre. Four days of feasting, frolicking, sports of all kinds, and long, lingering hangovers from the sweet but strong winter ales and hot, spiced wine. On the first day, as the braziers were lit, stalls set up and decorations made from winterberry, mistletoe and larkspur, a large, restless bear was seen pacing the path across the river. Bears were not unusual, but tended to keep to the great woods where food was abundant, avoiding unpredictable human encounters. We should have known it was an omen.

Townspeople went about their preparations, with one wary half eye on the far bank where the beast shuffled back and forth as if contemplating its next move, deterred from crossing partly, it seemed, by the ice that thinned to nothing at the rivers centre.

Soon they were distracted by aromas of roasting chestnut, mulled cider and buns freshly baked with cinnamon, nutmeg and brown sugar. Anticipation rose too for games that were about to begin. Coloured ribbons marked out courses for the ski chase, the skating race on the frozen lake, and the snow run to the wood's edge and back. Pride and honours came with victory in these, but the crowd shouted as much at annual favourites, the icy pole climb and the cold bath pit pull. To make the pole, the previous night, hardy volunteers tipped water over a trimmed tree trunk leaving it until hard and deep crusted with ice. Competitors would clamber as fast as they could to its slippery 18 foot height to grab a holly crown. The pit pull was a tug of war either side of an ice-filled pond, the losers allowed to sit closest to the burning braziers and slowly steam dry.

All gathered in a slightly shivering giant circle in the town square for the midday Saining, the blessing. To drive away evil spirits and begin the Fayre, juniper branches were burned and blessed water drunk, drawn from the river ford believed a crossing for both living and dead.

Cups were lifted as bells tolled eight, nine, ten... commotion, rustling from the side nearest the river... eleven... shrieks, gasps and stumbling as the crowd parted and a huge bear ambled into view. And what was its expression, could it be that the animal was half smirking?

After the shock, silence. Cold already, now frozen to the spot. A flindrikin of light snow had turned into flukra, large flakes falling.

"Don't look so worried," it said, to even greater consternation, "I've come to help you, not hurt you. I ask nothing in return," with a wide open gesture of giant, gentle seeming paws.

"You all seem cold, I know where the best firewood is, and buried beneath the forest there are magical rocks and a liquid, dark as starless sky, that can burn and warm you." Then the bear bid us go about our festivities, promising it would later guide us to these places. Dubiously at first, the town agreed.

That winter indeed proved to be cold, like one endless hoolie, a freezing gale that saw snow feefle round every corner, blin drifts against every house such that we seemed endlessly to be digging out our neighbours. And even when the wind fell, great skelf flakes fell, layer upon layer, flattening everything, silencing the land. We felt like an ice world version of Pompeii, imagining some future traveller with cause to dig would stumble across our frozen forms and wonder what had happened here. Those still hardy enough to ski, skate and stomp (the snow being too deep to run) spent hours returning life to their frost bitten fingers and toes.

Little surprise then, that after the games, the townspeople followed the bear to the best firewood, and discovered the abundant rocks and liquid that burned with such heat. Soon every house had new lamps and stoves that seemed permanently lit and fires never went out. At night the walls of homes pulsed with warmth as if the stone had soaked up days of midsummer sun. Clouds of light soot suspended in the air seemed a small price to pay. As it coloured with black specks, the drifts beginning to melt from the heat, children started calling it snirt, for dirty snow. The bear was sighted once or twice more across the river, watching with what might have been a smile to see its good works or, I wondered, that smirk for some other reason.

My own children grew. Three years passed and at the Frost Fayre my eldest, Dawn, in her prime, won the ski race, beating all the young men of the town, to their collective embarrassment and indignation. Yet, they did not see how she had trained. Not just the hours early in the morning when she would return, every muscle aching and damp with sweat, but how she studied and knew the land. Or, how carefully she prepared and waxed her skis, and how in the evening, when all tasks were done and the men were in the ale house, she would take the heavier fire logs, lift and twist with them in every imaginable way, until every part of her was sinewy, as strong and firm as an ox, though she was agile as a deer.

Her prize was to lead the traditional walk of light that ended the Fayre. Fire balls fashioned from wicker and swung on sticks were symbols of the power of the sun to rid evil. The procession finished at the river where they were floated on small rafts slowly consumed by flames. Only one comment lingered that year. The snow runners complained that since all the tree felling and mining, it was now much further to run to the forest's edge. The wish-hunt for Arctic hare went off, but though its footsteps were found, it was not seen.

Three years later, Dusk too entered her prime. Like Dawn, she beat all the young men to win the long distance lake skate. All agreed that none could match her technical perfection and extraordinary endurance, built from hours and hours of hypnotic practice that often left her feet blistered and bleeding, and toes without nails. But, for the first time, it had to be held far north of the town, as the local lake would no longer freeze hard enough. That was not the only change. Except for sorry piles of sludgy snirt by roadsides, the town itself was almost free of snow. And it was thin, too, across the fields that stretched much farther before the runners could reach the forest's edge.

Some began to talk, quietly cursing the constant cloud of smoke around their homes. Now, if you couldn't see people, you could often hear them coughing. But there was light, heat, and always new contraptions that could be powered by the burning oil. Some in town were rumoured to meet with the bear in the woods, who told them of new places to find more. Those who raised and transported the plunder from earth were making money, building larger houses with more fireplaces, lamps and other hungry contraptions.

When you are living through something, change creeps up on you such that at first it is hard to see. This, I think, is how it was for the townsfolk. There were signs, and people grumbled, but few connected the slow decline of our well-being and the place we called home with the path that the bear had so slyly set us upon.

Now we come to the year of my sadness. It began at the Fayre twelve months ago. My third daughter, Midnight, was born quiet, like the sleeping hours, but she was a watcher. It seemed not only that she could see in the dark, but that she could see the dark around her, and in people. Midnight had long known something was very wrong in Skovin, I had felt the disquiet in her. I knew also that she was a child of great resolve, but I did not know that secretly she had fashioned a plan. She was known locally as the 'walker', for her endless wandering and exploring. She seemed to inhale the world around her, drink in the ways of nature, as if storing her knowledge like preserved fruit for a time of hardship. And, now was a time of difficulty, one that we had brought on ourselves.

Everyone expected her to win the snow walk, though little snow there was and it did not even begin for more than a mile towards the ever receding forest. Nobody understood why, after setting off and quickly leaving her fellows lagging behind, she was never seen again.

Search, oh how we, her sisters and I searched. How I pestered the people of our town to join in looking. Concerned and helpful at first, soon they became reluctant, grumbling to be away from their new comforts. It was pointless, they said. A wolf had taken her, they said. Or something else. But I never gave up. A parent doesn't.

At the edge of the forest Midnight turned momentarily, barely breathing, to see the others lurching slowly up behind, faces down, hands pushing on thighs against the incline. Then she slid from the track, marked with ribbons, and disappeared into the dark wood. It wasn't a wolf that took her, but her own determination. She would find the truth and how to return the snow. Emerging from the first great wood onto a higher plateau where the air was still cold enough to shock her lungs and the ground was once again white, she saw them: small but distinct, regular marks in the snow.

She checked her pockets for the food she had hidden – years of long walks taught her what was essential – for the rest, her knowledge of plants and foraging would be enough. Focused, with eyes like a snow owl, moving at more than a walk, less than a run, she hushed over the ground, hopped roots and rocks, jumped over hollows, ducked under branches until the day was gone and a luminous pale blue glowed equally everywhere. She heard her breath, her own heart, the night animals and soft crunch of her steps. Always she followed in the hare's footsteps, and she did not stop.

Was it three hours, six, or mesmerised, had it been whole nights and days? But then, in the dark, she saw what looked like two tiny moons rise above a crest. "Snawghast," she whispered, the ghost in the snow, their name for the white hare with its ears like twin apparitions.

"You come from Skovin, the town of smoke and things, that once just went about life, kept house and amused itself with sport." It was not a question. Turning impassively, but perhaps with a hare's ear-flick of concern to face Midnight, the Snawghast just seemed to know.

"You are under the spell of the bear. I know you alone see that and it is why you have come, to ask a wish of me to free you from it. But what you don't know is that the bear too is possessed, and to free yourselves you must set it free." Midnight knew this to be true as soon as the words were spoken. She listened to the impossible things that would have to be done for the remotest hope of success.

The almost impossible, that carried no guarantee, took a year.

Skovin glowed in the land beneath a brown smog like the embers of a building recently burned down but still smoking. It was the time of our games again, now a sad, polluted caricature of the pristine Frost Fayres already slipping from memory. Somehow in maintaining our traditions we were able to pretend to ourselves that nothing, really, was wrong.

Yet our lungs were sick. The fields were sick. The trees diseased. Animals coughed and staggered, few grew to maturity. Any life left in the river gasped, near its last. And I was still bereft. The faded Fayre's opening evening charade approached. A rough-hewn platform at its centre that served as a kind of wooden throne for our benefactor bear who came each year to look, or leer, at the changes he had wrought. It was late and I had not the patience, was turning to leave when a neighbour said, flatly, "Midnight approaches..." I began to correct him with, "It is not so late..." then I followed the neighbours line of sight and saw his meaning was different.

"Mother!" my daughter cried in a flurry like the snow of old, "Quick we have no time..." Her words now like a blizzard.

"It is the bear, but not the bear, that has done all this. It is possessed of a most evil spirit, *Droch Sluagh*, vengeful of our human form, our joy and play, and bent on drawing us to our own humiliation and destruction." My eyes widened, it was strange enough merely to see Midnight again. Joy curdled with foreboding as she spoke...

"What you see already is bad, but the spirit is capable of far worse. While it occupies the heart of the bear, taking animal form gives it untold powers. The swipe of a paw may trigger a conflagration in the heavens that can leave whole towns, valleys as ash. It must be stopped."

She spoke so fast about what had come to pass in the last year that my heart beat as if I myself had raced the length of our land, but this is what I understood.

As a cub, when weakened and ashamed, the bear was inhabited by the spirit. The cub had been unable to save its parents, shot by hunters who wrongly thought them guilty of killing livestock. *Droch Sluagh* mingled with the cub's grief and rage at humans till it was breathed in unnoticed. Then, as evil spirits do, it used its cunning for its own perverse sport, to cajole the humans to self-destruction. Midnight learned from the Snawghast that this very evening of our games the spirit planned its terrible, theatrical coup. Unless...

On its wooden throne the bear sat waiting to be garlanded, an honoured guest. A new game of wrestling had been suggested to open the games, designed especially for the bear to win. Snow and ice were now all but irrelevant. But first, it seemed, the bear was to be anointed in a ritual throwback to some half-forgotten ceremony. The bear, or rather the spirit, grinned to see these ingratiating humans bestow gifts, unknowingly, on their nemesis.

In a cloak and hood decorated with soot-edged leaves and berries (there were no others) one of the villagers solemnly stepped forward.

"Great bear, we welcome and bless you with the offerings of our land."

With that, the figure took three things from the cloak's deep pockets. In the bear's body, the *Droch Sluagh* oozed with amused self-satisfaction.

"We give your lips precious balm, made of rare herbs from the first leaves of spring, so that your smile may glisten like a meadow in dew," and with that fingers delicately smeared balm around the bear's mouth, the bear almost purring. What else would a vain spirit that was more in love with itself than Narcissus do?

"We bless your head with water from the first snow to melt in summer on the peak of Mount Smoor," and the bear's head was jewelled with droplets.

"We honour your feet with powder from plants harvested beneath a blood moon," and a fine dust was blown on to the bear's paws and the ground around where it sat.

For a brief moment, *Droch Sluagh* pondered how long it should wait before invoking fiery calamity to create maximum dramatic effect. One second, two, three – what would be most entertaining before the bodies fled and fell in flames?

Before there was time to complete its thought, the spirit felt at first a mild tingling on its inhabited bear's lips, as if it had chewed on a ginger root. Then the fur on its head began to itch, just before its paws became hot as if it had trodden in the still warm embers of a fire. Distraction became alarm when its mouth quickly raged as if it had bitten into the hottest chillies, and the gap between its ears like lightning had struck. The ground now seemed to be on fire.

Fearfully all but one of townspeople drew back from the bear, which now was twisting and lurching unnaturally, and howling like a storm at sea. Only the cloaked figure who gave the blessing remained, removing its hood to reveal Midnight, who cried, "*Droch Sluagh* you have tormented this beast and my town long enough. The Snawghast taught me to weave the seasons' gifts over one whole year to defeat you. But the only way to win was for you to welcome your own destruction, just as you tricked these people nearly to welcome theirs. I have smudged you with the sage of spring growth that drives out bad spirits, showered you in sacred mountain waters that signal the coming abundance of life, and dusted you with henbane and mandrake that expel evil. A trickster tricked by its own vanity and conceit."

Like something between a mountain vomiting and a barn burning to the ground, black smoke hissed from the bear, which slumped, unconscious.

I ran to Midnight's side. As she turned, shock at what she'd done dissolving the ice-hard determination in her look, a single snowflake fell down through the dissipating smog and landed on her cheek.

Héctor's journey: could footballers save the planet?

Freddie Daley

As societies face up to the realities of a warming world, there is a simmering sense that our past experiences are by no means a guide for our future. Uncertainties abound. And a compelling vision of the future – whatever shape it might arrive in – is acutely lacking. What's clear, though, is that the impacts of climate change will increasingly shape our lives in unpredictable and unforeseen ways, pulling at the fabric of communities and economies.

Who will help us navigate this future? And how will we get there? The hope of elected politicians filling this role is, quite frankly, for the birds. The policy target that pervades Western democracies is one of 'net zero', whereby its comforts, consumption patterns and privileges are sustained through electrification.

Climate breakdown is a technological problem with technological solutions.

This future looks much like the present. There are, of course, a couple of minor adjustments and slight inconveniences, but we will probably not notice it arriving. This is a future in which the vast majority of people will see no benefit or improvement; where current inequalities and injustices, those local and global, are re-cast in a green sheen. It is a future that is not worth fighting for, but also, because it is blind to a range of other planetary boundaries being transgressed due to the overconsumption of the wealthy, it is also unrealistic and impossible to deliver.

Filling this imaginative void and creating a compelling image of the future is an urgent endeavour. And it requires *culture* to sketch its contours, crystallise the stories and folklore that might underpin it, and move people emotionally and spiritually. Football, as one of the largest collective cultural phenomena on earth besides religion, has a part to play. Its gods – the women and men who can play the game at the highest levels – could be cultural cartographers, mapping a future worth fighting for.

When I think about this – which is often – I always come back to Héctor Bellerín. The Barcelona-born footballer who joined the Arsenal youth academy in 2011, aged 16. Having parted ways with the prestigious La Masia youth academy at Barcelona FC, Bellerin chose to make North London his home in a bid for regular first team football.

Before his arrival, rumours swirled. This isn't unusual. Surrounding every football transfer there is always an incessant churn of chatter and hearsay, which sometimes verges on fantasy. But Bellerín was purported to have pace – and had apparently broken the sprint record set by Arsenal's very own Theo Walcott. Already, he was being woven into the mythology of the club.

It didn't take long for Bellerín to impress and, in 2013, he got the call up to the first team. Almost immediately, he carved out a role at right back and cultivated an intimidating reputation within the Premier League for his pace, positional understanding, and tackling – a desirable trinity for right-backs in the modern era of football. Off the pitch, he quickly became a celebrity. Sitting front row at London Fashion Week, there were countless collaborations with brands and fashion houses, and magazine photoshoots and interviews in which Bellerín spoke candidly about the world around him. Football was always central, but it was an anchor dropped amid a messy, chaotic and unjust world.

These public interventions – which continue to this day – offer us a rare window to explore the role of footballers and, by extension, athletes as activists and social commentators on the unfolding climate crisis. Through every interview, we got to witness Héctor reckon with himself. His privilege as a wealthy, white footballer. His positionality as an influential public figure, embedded within social networks that bridge the physical and the digital, and stretch around the globe. And his multiplicity, where his various roles – as a professional footballer, a citizen with a voice and vote, and a human being enmeshed into the web of life – gave rise to tensions that he embraced, wholeheartedly and unashamedly.

Héctor's time in North London wasn't all smiles and high-fashion though. Problems began to mount as he came to be relied upon extensively at right-back by his team during the 2018-2019 season and, in the absence of any rotation, his body began to protest. During the early exchanges of a London derby against Chelsea, in January 2019, Héctor pulled up and then dropped to the grass. The anterior cruciate ligament (ACL) in his left knee had ruptured – the great fear of footballers everywhere – and he knew, instantly, that it was serious.

What followed was surgery and then a lengthy period of recovery, spanning almost nine months. This period of his life was fastidiously documented and shared online, followed by millions. Throughout these videos, Héctor laid bare the frustrations of not being able to play the game he loved and had dedicated his life to. The audience is granted glimpses of the monotony of recovery; the slow, repetitive movements, the litany of tiny setbacks, and the simmering exasperation that comes when your body fails to do what it has always done – your agency suspended because of a few millimetres of connective tissue.

Throughout this series, and the interviews he gave during this period, Héctor speaks with honesty and integrity about his struggles; the toll the injury has taken on his mental health, his subsequent battle with alcoholism, and the constant barrage of online hate he faced. These moments are deeply human and, at times, private. The audience is spared nothing: we all bear witness to the heavy pauses and the moments of introspection.

But introspection is never a one-way street. By going into yourself, you are forced to open up to the world around you and, by extension, your place in it. From the mid-2010s onwards, Héctor began to speak out prolifically and publicly on matters beyond football. Time and time again, he used his platform to draw attention to the multi-faceted and intertwined challenges facing humanity. From racial and gender equality, to the rights of refugees and the need to empower young people, there was no topic in which he held his tongue, nor an issue where he felt unprepared to offer his thoughts. His interventions were intersectionality in practice, using his platform and words to thread together shared suffering.

More frequently, though, Héctor spoke out on the intertwined climate and ecological crisis that is unfurling before our eyes. Living more sustainably has, in his own words, "always been a big thing" that is weaved through every decision he makes, a touchpoint for him to navigate daily life.[9] He cycles to work, eats plant-based food, and frequents public transport

---

9   Hector Bellerin at Real Betis: Championing sustainability and tackling social issues – BBC Sport, February 2024.

over the supercars and SUVs favoured by his peers. Despite these individual actions, Héctor's approach is deeply political: "we have a great opportunity every time we vote that we can make sure we create a more sustainable future".[10]

At the top of the men's game, Héctor remains an anomaly. But why? Climate breakdown is not the only crisis we face. For some, like the middle-classes of the Global North, it is perhaps the most visceral – especially given the increasing frequency of its impacts. But for billions of people around the world – professional footballers included – there are more immediate threats, to themselves, their communities and their aspirations. Climate catastrophe is but another catastrophe layered on top for a deep geological record of injustice, wrongdoing, and suffering.

Black footballers continue to face racism from the stands and terraces. These players have demanded change for decades, and still racism is packaged up as a problem that they themselves must counter, rather than societal malfeasance. Female footballers at the top of the game are grossly underpaid, compete on pitches that would never make the cut in the men's game, and are facing an epidemic of injuries due to playing in a professional game shaped by, and for, men. The experiences of these groups of players are by

---

10   Ibid

no means comparable, but they indicate the variety of threats footballers face that may supersede concerns over technical issues such as emissions cuts.

Speaking out too comes with risks. The relationship between professional footballers and the media has an ugly history. Héctor concedes himself that 'cancel culture' and an unforgiving media landscape can cause hesitancy amongst would-be athlete activists.[11] He himself has fallen prey to tabloid newspapers decrying his stances on social issues as the meaningless posturing of 'champagne socialists' and being continuously told to "stick to football", as if the game insulated you from experiencing the world around you, numbing your ability to tell which way the wind is blowing. Countless times he was labelled a 'hypocrite' for speaking out on the urgency of addressing the climate crisis, and the role which we can all play, on account of his wealth and celebrity.

Footballers fear the charge of hypocrisy – and with good reason. Public opinion polling in the UK emphasises a deep-rooted and persistent distaste towards hypocrites. The public discourse that often surrounds international climate conferences or inter-governmental gatherings, such as the annual Conference of the Parties (COP) and the G20 group of nations, reflects this. Antagonism is hurled towards those decision-makers and powerful members of the

---

11   Ibid.

elite for saturating the sky with private jets in the name of protecting the environment.

But when footballers are tarred with the same brush, there is a conflation between real power and agency over the trajectory humanity charts in the decades ahead, and a softer form of power; a blend of celebrity and cultural influence, alongside leverage with brands, sporting institutions and, sometimes, policy makers (see influential British footballer, Marcus Rashford, for example). The former group defines what feasible climate action is and the guardrails of climate leadership, while the latter can only hope to raise awareness of the threats posed and normalise the actions we all need to take.

How, then, could footballers save the planet? In multiple ways. Like all of us, footballers are individuals that encounter and interact with multiple systems and are embedded in complex networks. And, like everyone else, footballers are both shaped by these systems while shaping them through their own actions and choices. But, unlike everyone else, footballers may have more ability to shape certain systems that they are part of and interact with, both as individuals and collectively. This is because footballers play many roles within and beyond sport due to the social, financial and cultural resources they hold.

Football is the world's biggest and most watched sport. Its athletes have unique power as worshipped public figures who could rapidly normalise different ways of behaving and living. In a single pre- or post-match press conference they could create a whole new conversation, say about whether to fly or not, or consign the reputation of a malign company to the bin of history. They can compel an otherwise easily bored or distracted audience to pay attention to anything from child poverty to systemic racism. This type of power cannot be underestimated in a warming world filled with injustice.

Héctor Bellerín will continue to inspire people simply by being himself, understanding his influence and speaking-up when given the space for those that are almost always excluded. The social and political life of Héctor Bellerín, and his continued commitment to advocating for a better world for every human, should offer us all solace that there is strength in vulnerability, influence in introspection and self-reflection, and solidarity and love when we speak out against what is wrong and what is right. This is why I often think about Héctor Bellerín.

Letter From Claremont: Mike Davis is Dying[12]

David Goldblatt

Indeed I live in the dark ages!
A guileless word is an absurdity. A smooth forehead
betokens
A hard heart. He who laughs
Has not yet heard
The terrible tidings.
Ah, what an age it is
When to speak of trees is almost a crime
For it is a kind of silence about injustice!
And he who walks calmly across the street,
Is he not out of reach of his friends
In trouble?
Bertolt Brecht, *On Posterity*

---

12   First published in Boom California, March 2023,
     https://boomcalifornia.org/2023/03/06/letter-from-claremont-mike-da-
     vis-is-dying/

September 2022, Claremont, CA

All through the blistering heatwave that has held Southern California in a vice, I've been thinking about Mike. Mike Davis is dying. Esophageal cancer that won't go away. Last month he opted for palliative care; the end can't be too far off. The heatwave has another three days to run. Here, in Claremont, it has been around 78 degrees at dawn, climbing to a long hot afternoon plateau as high as 110. I could drive, air-con blazing, to other air-conditioned spaces, but even the short walks across searing hot car parks are unpleasant. Not so much the heat itself, but the deep sense it communicates, that something is very wrong.

I feel it, I think, somewhere deeper than the conscious mind, somewhere buried in the ancient brain stem that stores our trauma and turns it into networks of toxic neurons. So, teaching and food shopping aside, I'm just bunkering down in Professor Davina's place with its clattering vintage air-con: yoga twice a day, a lot of stillness, just breathing, being in my creaky body... and thinking about Mike.

Mike Davis is one of my guiding stars. I've read everything he has ever written, much of it twice. When in 1991, as a grad student in England, I picked up *City of Quartz*, his polycentric history of Los Angeles, and I couldn't put it down. I was captivated by its account of the city's illusions and mythologies, alongside the realities of its racist policing and its fortified architecture. I couldn't believe sociology or history or theory (it intuitively shape-shifts) could be so smart and sassy, so sharp and stylish, saying it like it is, but wow, saying it like Raymond Chandler. Turns out Mike hates Chandler, for his misogyny, his racism, his small-minded individualism and his amoral fatalistic fascism, but he also can't stop reading him. I can't stop reading Mike, and though I've never met him, I have at least walked in his footsteps. Back in the 1990s, during one of his many periods of financial difficulty and professional limbo, he came and taught at Pitzer college. And I have done much the same. In over a decade of living in and exploring Los Angeles he has been my constant guide and made this strange but extraordinary metropolis at least comprehensible.

A lot of writers might have just left it there. Whole academic careers have been sustained on slighter contributions than *City of Quartz*, but Mike was a late starter. A meat cutter, trucker and trade union activist in his late teens and twenties, he didn't show up at UCLA for his degree until he was 30. Impressive as the book was, it was mere prelude, the curtain raiser to two decades of superhuman scholarship and activism. *Magical Urbanism* surveys the Latino transformation of the American city and its progressive political and aesthetic potential. *Planet of Slums*, by contrast, was a cadastral survey of the informal settlements that house more than three billion people, in the mega cities of the twenty-first century. *Buda's Wagon* was a short and brilliant history of the car bomb and asymmetrical warfare, from Italian-American anarchists to al-Qaeda. *Mid Victorian Holocausts* is a masterpiece of environmental history, explaining the origins of the global south at the intersection of Victorian imperialism and the El Nino weather events of the era that generated famines, deaths and environmental degradation of such a scale that the gap between North and South became a chasm. In *The Monster to Come*, a short essay on coronaviruses, avian flu and epidemiology in an era of globalisation, published in 2009, he accurately predicted the emergence and course of the COVID pandemic. I could go on.....and on.

His third book, *Ecology of Fear* sits on my desk. I feel right now like I'm not reading it but living it. So, I'm lucky that Professor Davina's house, where miraculously I have landed, is a good antidote. Born in the rural Philippines in the 1920s, she arrived in California in her forties and lived here for nearly half a century. For thirty years she was the first Filipina professor of theology in California, teaching at Chaffey Community College. I drink my tea out of a college mug saying "we're here to help". The last couple of decades she was retired and mainly alone; three kids who had moved on and a second husband, Milt, who died fifteen years ago. Professor Davina died last year, and her daughter Dodi just didn't have it in her to sort and clear the house: grief, Covid, losing her own partner just three months after her mother, and then breast cancer and surgery. So, the house has sat empty until I arrived, part caretaker, part tenant.

There are still a few reminders of Davina's last couple of years—walkers gathering dust, mobility aids in her bathroom—but it's the rest of her long life that is really present. Dodi told me she had tried to clear some away, but the house is crammed with ecumenical knick- knacks: a seder plate on the wall above the kitchen table, inspirational quotes from a Native American shaman on grubby fridge magnets, statuettes of Confucius and the Buddha, a chopping board from the United Methodists Church, Hindu figurines, Islamic banners. In her office and the living room a lifetime of study, encyclopaedias of comparative religion, bibles, Korans, torahs....

One pleasing quirk of the house is the absence of plastic. Dodi said, "She was an environmentalist before her time. She hated plastic." Look around, the house is full of wood and ceramics, textiles and glass, bamboo, rattan and metal, but literally no plastic. She preferred bone handled knives and wicker basket bins, and all in shades of white and beige and brown and bronze. Clingfilm was allowed, as a cupboard of maybe a dozen huge rolls testifies, but only as an alternative to using Tupperware. Sure, her computer kit and TV are plastic, but I sense they were not much loved. On the shelves in her office there are, carefully organized and catalogued, the products of old analogue technologies—cameras in leather cases, teaching slides in cardboard boxes dozens of photo albums, and half dozen metal rolodexes. On the inside of the food cupboard is an old, typed list, probably from the 1980s, of small environmental actions that we might take—use what you buy, write on both sides of your note paper, choose the lesser of two evils. Its tone is humble and practical, and although the advice feels hopelessly inadequate, it's a better voice to listen to than my own sense of creeping doom.

It helps make the house a good place to hide from the heat through the long afternoons. Conscious of the antiquity of the air conditioning system—and the impossibility of getting it repaired right now—I try and nurse it, keeping the thermostat at 71 degrees, but as the sun passes from the front of the house over the roof and into the back garden it can't keep up. The internal temperature climbs and climbs and I find myself dozing uneasily on the sofa, unable to move. Yesterday my siesta was broken by a series of noisy, unignorable urgent sounds from my British and American cell phones. It's a text from California's energy agencies letting us now that the level of demand for electricity is reaching breakpoint. If, for the next few hours, we don't all turn off everything short of the AC then we are looking at rolling outages and blackouts. I turn out the lights, leave my washing and cooking to later, light a few of the professor's devotional candles and get back to Mike and *Ecology of Fear*.

The book's basic premise is that to build a metropolis of nearly fifteen million people in a desert is not sustainable. Make it exclusively dependent on the private motor car, and you are really in trouble. Add the fire hazards on the wooded slopes of Los

Mike Davis at a volcano in Hawaii. By Alessandra Moctezuma

Angeles' hills and mountains, and the insatiable demand for water that simply isn't there and disaster looms. Now factor in another two decades of climate change since the book was written and the city, right now, is close to unlivable and only so at the price of more massive carbon emissions.

Then there is the San Andreas fault, the geological atom bomb that runs through the greater Los Angeles metropolitan area. Tremors are a dime a dozen here, though as I know from my own quivering disbelief on experiencing one, no less unnerving for that. The last time the fault really bared its teeth was the Northridge Earthquake in 1994. It is, by historic standards, due to do so again, sometime soon. Professor Davina had been making preparations. In the garage, beneath a dusty bunch of yellow plastic roses, I find the remnants of a basic earthquake stash—eight big plastic bottles of water, torches, batteries, first aid kit. I'm not sure any of it will be much use when the big one comes and make a mental note to assemble my own.

I sit inside nearly all day. After about 1:00pm the sun has passed over the front of the house, and outside the front door there is a small pool of hot shade. The small park opposite is entirely empty. For a couple of hours after dawn there is a smattering of dog walkers and determined joggers, but then there is no one until dusk. Huge SUVs, sparkling white and black and silver, occasionally glide past. I listen to the rumble of the 210 freeway, just a hundred metres north of us, the hum of my neighbour's air conditioner, watch the vapour trails of planes heading to and from LAX.

Only as the sun is going down do I make my way to the back garden. It's still fearsomely hot, but at least I can look at the smog rainbow sunset and the San Gabriel Mountains. In past summers there still would have been a sprinkling of snow on the high peaks, but they are brown and bare. The smog is still with us. I can see that once the garden was a beautiful space with pomegranate, cherry and apricot trees and dozens of fabulous huge succulents. Since Professor Davina died, the drip hoses and sprinklers have broken and there has been no watering at all. Southern California is in the midst of an unprecedented three-year long drought, so there hasn't been much help from the weather. Now the apricot and cherry trees are dead, their few remaining leaves are crisped to a dark brown. The succulents, still just hanging on, have shrunk, and shrivelled and shed what leaves they have held onto to survive. But they are a sorry sight—desiccated mutant versions of themselves. The pomegranate has, amazingly, hung on, and is even bearing fruit. I can't bear to pick them. It seems, after such herculean botanical efforts, too cruel to take it. Dodi has arranged for landscapers to take out the dead, put in new drips and drought resistant plants, maybe save the pomegranate and the succulents. I tend and water my little collection of newly potted tomatoes and basil. They are surviving.

It doesn't take much to join the dots here. But as the news from home, where the government is arresting people demanding that the country's ageing housing be fitted with better insulation suggests, the economic and political elites of this world are willfully refusing to do so. I'm reading Mike again, in what will probably be his last interview, and, as ever, he condenses my thoughts, and finds words to pierce my heart.

"Our ruling classes everywhere have no rational analysis or explanation for the immediate future. A small group of people have more concentrated power over the human future than ever before in human history, and they have no vision, no strategy, no plan."

So, what to do? On one of the many occasional tables scattered around Professor Davina's house, alongside a carved wooden cockerel from the Philippines and a dusty menorah, lies a small, cardboard oval. It is threaded with old string for hanging on a wall, but it has been left on the table. I didn't notice it for the first week I was here. Then, for no reason at all, I stopped and looked at it. In thick embossed silver script it says "hope". It's kitsch and it's corny, but right now I'll take corny.

Last week at a press conference, PSG star Kilian Mbappe and coach Christophe Galtier were asked why the team took a private jet from Paris to Nantes, just a few hundred kilometres away and accessible by TGV. They both laughed. Galtier quipped, "This morning we talked about it with the company which organises our trips and we're looking into travelling on sand yachts." I showed it to my students. It was electric. For the next forty minutes we explored how sports are connected to the climate crisis and what it might do about it. The power and responsibilities of athletic celebrity, the inequality of carbon emissions and climate impacts, football in Africa in a heating world, how climate change affected their own play (lots of them are on the college soccer team), and a dozen other things. They were a mix of amazed, curious, angry—and ignited. For all the detail, what was really going on was the sound of hundreds of pennies dropping; the slot machine of education hitting the jackpot.

Afterwards, thinking about Mbappe laughing and his smooth ephebic forehead, I made the connection back to Brecht. Of course, it was Mike, whose breadth of reading has never ceased to amaze and please me,

Pomona , Cal.; Claremont and Old Baldy. By Brück & Sohn Kunstverlag Meißen

that got me back to *On Posterity*. In the time left to him, he says he's doing a lot of family time, watching Scandinavian noir and reading Brecht. He said:

"I've always been influenced by the poems Brecht wrote in the late 30s, during the Second World War, after everything had been incinerated, all the dreams and values of an entire generation destroyed, and Brecht said, 'Well, it's a new dark ages....how do people resist in the dark ages?'"

Brecht, in the end, offers pretty thin gruel. He knows it and asks us, "Do not judge us too harshly." I need more than that. Mike Davis, for me, just nails it, "Despair is useless."

What keeps us going, ultimately, is our love for each other, and our refusal to bow our heads, to accept the verdict, however all-powerful it seems. It's what ordinary people have to do. You have to love each other. You have to defend each other. You have to fight.

So, I'm writing this and sending it to you because I love you (and Mike Davis, and Professor Davina, and my Pitzer college students), and I'm trying not to bow my head, and to find my way to be a part of our mutual defiance, for what I'm worth. If you want to fight, I'm all ears, but love is also allowed, and if you want to go read some Mike Davis, then that's good too.

Coda

Mike Davis left us in late October. The heatwave gave way to a long hot autumn, and then the cataclysmic storm and rains of late December 2022 and early January 2023. Professor Davina's house held up and Dodi and I have made a start on sifting and sorting it.

What's an 'Ology got to do with sport?

Mark Perryman

In 1983 as a fresh-faced youth (back then I still had hair) I bought and read Garry Whannel's pioneering book, *Culture, Politics and Sport: Blowing the Whistle*. It was part of an *Arguments for Socialism* series from the left wing publisher Pluto. I was on the left – and still am – and had been sports-mad but I had kind of given up most of my sport for the cause. After reading Garry's five point manifesto of how to understand sport, this all changed:

- **First,** there is a need to take all aspects of social life seriously, especially popular cultural forms like sport.

- **Second**, recognise that sport contributes to the way people see the world, engage and offer alternatives.

- **Third**, physical well-being, health and fitness are important to human development.

- **Fourth**, play in some form will be an important element of a more fulfilling society.

- **Fifth**, leisure will become an increasingly politicised issue, battles will be fought over who has leisure time, how it is spent and how it is provided for.

And to summarise, Garry set out brilliantly the context he and others were up against:

"Sport is marked down as a natural, taken-for-granted activity. You don't need to talk or write about it. You just do it."

A year later I wrote my first article on sport for the magazine *Marxism Today* arguing how mass participation city marathons were a model for democratisation vs marketisation of physical activity. I've hardly stopped writing on the politics of sport since.

But there was another reason I'd given up doing sport. At University I found pretty much the entire sports culture both highly regimented and fiercely competitive. My sport was middle and long distance running. I competed but the appeal was to run on my own, to train myself, to set my own targets. None of this fitted with the dominant ethos of university sports clubs, an ethos that is central to putting most people off sport.

Contrast this to the 2010s. Wiggo, Hoy, Pendleton and Trott, Froome and Thomas , Team GB , Team Sky and the cycling boom they helped spark. But this wasn't just about elite success, the so-called 'role model' factor. Crucially cycling is the one sport we can use as means to get to work, it is fairly gender unspecific, open to young and old, as a family, relatively cheap, offers an informal competitive side, is often linked to charity/good causes, and is becoming aspirational/fashionable.

Jackie Ashley in the *Guardian* wasn't alone in dubbing 2012 'The Year of Cycling' while at the same time pointing to some of the messy contradictions that remain:

"A quarter of us, roughly, are obese, children as well as adults. Our urban air is filthy. We are using too much carbon. But the great thing is millions of us are getting the message. Real revolutions come from below, and this one is too. That's perhaps the greatest message from 2012, the year of the bike."

So why does Great Britain still have amongst the lowest cycling participation rates in all of Europe. Road safety, bike security, cultural attitudes, unintegrated transport system, work facilities all contribute.

In the early 1980s it was the running boom that was making similar headlines to cycling three decades later. Accompanied by the success of British runners Coe, Ovett, Cram and Elliott on the track, jogging became a social phenomenon, the first London marathon was run and almost every city and town could boast a fun run of sorts, many raising funds for good causes. In the USA Jim Fixx's *Complete Book of Running* became a bestseller, pretty soon with a worldwide readership too. Running had previously been something for serious, elite athletes, but it was rapidly becoming democratised – and ordinary people began to buy running shoes and think they could have a go too.

I was one of those. The first Olympics I can properly remember, Munich '72, was a Games of Team GB disappointment on the track. With his Zapata moustache, trademark red socks and a cockiness that we traditionally didn't associate with our Olympians, David Bedford was going to Munich to win, telling us back home to "stop what you are doing to watch me win a gold medal". He never even came close, despite attempting the same double as Mo triumphed in at the 2012 Games and 2013 World Championships: Dave finished sixth in the 5000m and a lowly twelfth in the 10,000m. A fantastic runner, just a year later Bedford was to run a world record time for the 10,000m, but at Munich he failed to live up to my boyhood expectations.

However, another runner did catch my eye: Dave Wottle, a US athlete who wore a battered old golf cap when he ran, symbolising an almost carefree attitude to his sport. He won 800m gold with a quite incredible sprint to the line from almost last position and forgot to take the cap off during the medal ceremony. Reviewing Wottle's career, the US magazine *Running Times* described his Munich victory as:

"Marking the end of the age of innocence for sport."

For me it was the beginning, and I hardly stopped

running since – until 2012 when I switched mostly to cycling, and more recently swimming.

In the 1980s, just like cycling today, running seemed to be part of a boom, and by the 1990s commentators were dubbing the era 'the Age of Sport'. Yet the twenty-first century has seen Britain with record levels of physical inactivity and obesity and all the health problems associated with both. Some run, cycle, swim too, but most don't.

Mark Rowlands is a philosopher of running and in his book *Running With the Pack* he makes two key observations of the sport. Firstly, for runners, what we do has a variety of purposes:

"Different people run for different reasons: some because they enjoy it, some because it makes them feel good, look good, because it keeps them healthy, happy – even alive. Some run for company, others to relieve the stress of everyday life. Some like to push themselves, test their limits; others to compare their limits with the limits of others."

But Mark then adds a second observation. That the appeal of running lies not in any of these reasons at all; the point of running is that it is pointless:

"It is true that running has multifarious forms of instrumental value. However, at its purest and its best running has an entirely different sort of value. This is sometimes known as 'intrinsic' or 'inherent' value. To say that something has intrinsic value is to say that it is valuable for what it is in itself, and not because of anything else it might allow to get or possess.

Running is intrinsically valuable, when one runs one is in contact with intrinsic value in life."

As I clock up another week's running and swimming mileage, I have come to realise all those years on from Dave Wottle and the Munich '72 Games that the appeal of an early morning run lies in that it has no purpose other than its appeal. Yes, my legs are stronger and fat-free, I can run a distance and a time plenty half my age couldn't even start. But the instrumentalism of running will always disappoint. I've scarcely ever won a race. Despite all those miles, I've still got a bigger waistline than I'd prefer. And running has left me less resistant to colds, flu and sundry other viruses.

So why do I run, cycle and swim? Because it's free and it is freedom; it is the most basic form of sporting activity. I run because I can.

And the reason I can is in large measure socially constructed. I have a lifestyle which enables me to put time aside most days for a run. I'm male, the dark mornings from October through to March don't hold too much fear for me. Today I live on the edge of the South Downs, so my gravest fear is that a randy bull takes an unnatural fancy to me. For twenty odd years though I ran along the towpath of the River Lea, circumnavigating what was to become the Olympic Park. In those two decades along my route there were two shootings, and on a couple of occasions I was chased by a variety of the deranged and the inebriated. Fortunately I have a decent finishing kick, which can come in useful when you least expect it.

And when I started my running, I went to a school with a playing field to run round that was next to a heath too. The basic facilities to nurture my childhood enthusiasm existed. I've never joined a running club; this is a sport you can do individually or collectively, but when I wanted to race there were events I could easily and cheaply enter, and I had family and friends to provide the transport and support I would sometimes rely upon.

And more latterly cycling? I am a commuter cyclist, so not much fear of traffic. Think Wiggomania, the Olympic Time Trial. Crucially *Le Tour* is free-to-watch on terrestrial TV. Brilliant commentary team. Le Tour '14 comes to Yorkshire, Tour of Britain. I'm fit, I enjoy testing my endurance. I can afford a decent bike and I'm surrounded by quiet country roads to ride down or up. And when I want to test myself, thanks to a network of Sussex Sportives, I can cycle a marked out route against the clock.

And swimming. In Lewes where I live we have a community-owned open air swimming pool, Pells Pool. It has cheap tickets, the unheated water provided by a natural spring. The space is divided between lanes for those who, like me, want to swim lengths, and the children and families who prefer a more unruly splash-about Pells. Or if it gets too crowded, Seaford beach is 15 minutes away by train. And in the winter months there's a Lewes indoor pool too.

I have come to value and protect the time I spend on my sport but in order to do so I had to have the time for sport in the first place. My access to sport is socially constructed. All sports are. For a precious few, doing sport will have changed their lives, but for most it hasn't. We can't keep society out of sport. Sport *is* social.

The last third of the run

Chris Nichols

There is always a point in a long run when my energy seems to fail. It's never in the last mile. Somewhere before that, the finish can start to feel a long way off. I have to decide to dig deeper or give up. When I get into the closing stages my energy picks up and I can finish with a sprint. That always feels good.

—

Energy, now that's an interesting word. I've always been blessed with lots of it. I supposed that's what makes me a runner – at least that's a story I tell myself. I've always loved the trails, the long paths, the cliff tops and beach runs. If I don't run, I'm miserable.

So, now I'm well into my sixties I decided to pick up the pace. My energy was waning, so I thought I'd treat life like I do in the last third of a run. Dig deeper, start to run some of the longer distances again that I'd stepped back from to protect my knees. And given my age, I thought, best to have a check-up, make sure that stepping up the running won't do me harm. So, I booked myself in.

I passed all the usual tests. Blood pressure bouncing along at the top of the healthy range, always has been. Blood fats a bit up, nothing to shout about but maybe worth a statin to keep your heart risk low, they told me.

"How confident do you want to be?" the cardiologist asks me, "we can be a bit more invasive and do a contrast CT, just to be sure". Why not, I thought.

—

"Well, that's a surprise" the doctor says, "you've got a severe narrowing of the most important artery feeding your heart. Are you sure you don't have any symptoms you've not told me about?".

So, more tests. A cardiac stress MRI, an invasive contrast angiogram through a catheter into an artery, a treadmill stress test ECG. All showing 100% normal blood flow.

"It's a conundrum," the cardiologist says," because with an artery like that you should be having symptoms, not running races".

So, what do we do, I ask. Is it time for stenting this, or a by-pass? I'm clear on this, I don't have symptoms and I do plan to keep running and trail walking. But I don't want my first symptom to be fatal, fifteen miles from the nearest phone signal.

"Here's the thing" the heart surgeon says, "we work on symptoms. If you don't have any that justify the surgery. Stenting can make the problem worse and by-pass surgery carries a risk of dying."

So, it's nothing for now. Carry on running, knowing that I have this troublesome artery, or ease off for good. Scale back the exercise and just take a stroll in the park? Maybe just put my feet up. It's been occupying my thoughts a lot since the diagnosis. Not in a debilitating way, but as a choice. What should I do?

—

I decided to keep going. My work is important to me. I love my customers and they love what we do. I decided to keep running too, and to increase my mileages. I've joined a running club again, to give me a bit of structure in increasing my training, and it's going well. The additional miles, the hills and the sprint work aren't causing any symptoms so far. I've cut out almost all alcohol. I've reduced the fat content of my diet, even more plant-based whole-foods, there is some evidence that the diet can help defer further worsening. I feel better for it, anyway.

And yes, it could all come crashing down. I can work hard, step up my miles, eat with discipline and rigour and it can still all go wrong in an instant. There's no guarantee at all that the blockage won't shift, and it may shift catastrophically. But I'm going to carry on, while I can.

—

I suppose how I feel about my heart is a bit like how I feel about our climate, and about all the damage done to the web of life support systems. The science is clear, but the symptoms aren't causing everyone to stop in their tracks. Are we going to ease back a bit? Or adopt radically different ways of living? Or will we carry on until the lifeblood of the planet stops flowing? Who knows?

For my part I'm going to keep on running and, for as long as I can, I'll keep doing work that helps people run their businesses in a way that makes sense for the earth. It's a small gesture, but it makes life better here and now, and it carries seeds of hope in it.

And I'll do it with love because that's what hope is, action done with love, without any certainty that it's going to win the day. Hope carries no guarantees at all, but if it's hope made with love it's all the better for it.

The trail's end

Caroline Staudt

On the morning of my 75th birthday, I woke up excited and nervous. Would my body hold up for the adventure I had planned? Would my grandchildren wish that they were at home doing anything but spending the day with their grandmother? But I knew that this day would be magical. I could smell the smells. I could see the colours. I could hear the leaves crunching under our feet. It had been years – decades – since I was last out in those woods, but now I had the opportunity to share them. A dream I had held onto for so long.

I left before dawn. After driving three hours, I arrived at my grandchildrens' house. At 9 and 11, they were starting to act like pre-teens, but so far they always remained polite to me. They gave me a quick hug and told me that they were excited to explore with me on my birthday. They had always enjoyed my stories about running in the woods. After a quick stop in the powder room and a second breakfast with their mom – my daughter – the three of us got in the car to start our adventure.

I started to feel my anticipation growing. I was finally taking my grandchildren back to the woods that had defined my young adulthood. The woods where I had spent countless hours running on trails.

I remember every tree. My favorites were always the maples and birches. The maples shone a brilliant scarlet colour in autumn which contrasted beautifully with the golden yellow of the birches. At the entrance to the trailhead, I remember that I could see two birches and three maples mixed in with the pine trees that were a predictable emerald no matter the time of year.

I remember every animal. On each run, I knew that I could count on seeing them. The insects, small and big, would fly in my face and, on hot runs, die on my sweat. The woodpeckers would reliably peck at the trees with a sound that echoed for hundreds of yards. I loved approaching them and quietly watching them work. It was almost as if they were frustrated humans banging their heads against a wall. It always made me laugh and wonder what they were thinking about. My heart still races when I think about the snakes. None of the snakes native to the woods are poisonous but having even a garter snake slither in front of me on a run was enough to stop my breath momentarily. And the deer. So often, I would run across deer and wind up in a staring contest that would only end when one of us ran away losing the game of chicken – usually me. The animals in my woods were not the most exotic, but, to me, they were always the most beautiful.

I remember the streams. They became icy in the winter turning even the easiest water crossings into an adventure. I never knew if the ice would hold my weight or if my feet would wind up numb. In the summer, the flowing water was a welcome respite. I would cool down my feet or my face when I needed a break. On the hottest days, I would even sit in the stream and soak my body for a few minutes. Once, I sat there so long taking in the sounds and smells that my fingers turned into prunes.

I told my grandchildren about all of it. The trees. The animals. The streams. I told them about my adventures running here while training for races that had me jet setting around the world. The people I used to run with. The way my body felt when I crested a large hill and the view came into focus. They had heard it all before, but they listened intently. I couldn't wait to show it to them. Our plan was to go for a grandmother-paced hike (my running days are behind me) along my favourite trail. I had run this trail hundreds of times and still felt confident that I knew every tree, rock, turn, and root, but I had not been back since I moved away 40 years ago.

Finally, after 2 hours in the car, we pulled into the parking lot. It was paved – that was different. But I took it as a sign of progress. It was also empty, which seemed unusual for a Saturday morning on a clear day. We made sure our shoes were tied, our water bottles were in our backpacks, and we each had snacks and a picnic lunch. I had even packed birthday cupcakes to surprise my grandchildren at my favourite picnic spot.

We opened the car door and the first thing that hit me was the smell. My woods smelled different. Gone was the fresh scent of pine. Instead, it smelled like a factory. Almost like oil. And ash. Dirty. I told the kids not to worry. Surely the smell of the trees would return once we got on the trail.

We walked towards the trailhead but it was gone. Not the whole trail but the trees that once created an elegant entrance. There were only stumps where my maples and birches used to be. The pines were gone too. I took a breath. I told myself that once we got around the first bend about 100 yards down the path, it would look like what I remembered. My grandchildren were hesitant, but I assured them that the woods I had described so many times would be just up ahead. We walked a little further. I could still follow the trail, but it was clear that no one had walked on this path in a long time. My heart raced.

It was quiet. I didn't hear any sounds from birds or deer or rustling leaves. I looked down. I saw a plastic water bottle. It looked old. Could that have been mine? When I was young and used to run these trails, I never did think twice about throwing my bottles and food wrappers down. None of us did. I shook off the feeling. That couldn't be my old bottle. The trees and the animal sounds must be just up ahead.

We kept walking. The sun was beating down. I realised that there was no shade. There was always shade. It was the woods. But it wasn't the woods. Not anymore. As far as the eye could see, there was evidence of fire. Evidence of logging. Evidence of drought. Evidence of runners and hikers who had been through here before. But no evidence of the things I remembered. No trees, just stumps and burnt logs. No streams, just empty gullies. No animals, just quiet. Not even the insects had survived in this place.

I turned away from my grandchildren. I didn't want them to see my face. What had I done? What had my generation done?

It's 'show time',
human race

Dave Hampton

It was August 1982, Lucerne, and it was race time. The final of the Men's Lightweight Eights was about to start; it was the Swiss' turn to host the annual World Rowing Championships, and the beautiful Rotsee lake seemed to know it. Nature seemed to know it. Even the ducks (in a ROW?) seemed to align. Maybe it was the crew's heightened senses, maybe it was in our nature.

Our cox was Pete Berners-Lee: brother to Tim, inventor of the internet, and brother to environmentalist Mike, author of 'How Bad are Bananas'.

At stroke was Robin Williams MBE (yes that one): at least 'that one' if you're thinking of the Robin who coached the legendary women's pair of Helen Glover and Heather Stanning to double Olympic Gold as champions in 2012 and 2016; and previously head coach to the Cambridge University Boat Club, for 11 years.

The crew comprised seasoned world champions and much talent, new and old. Two of the crew were tall heavyweights who had dieted dramatically over the season to lose several stone to make the weight.

Lightweight rowing had only been added to the World Rowing Championships programme back in 1974 for men, and 1985 for women. There was a shameful lack of parity then, even open-weight women were not added to the Olympic programme until 1976, despite open men's events since 1900. In the 1970s, British lightweight eights had set the bar high – winning gold in 1977, 1978 and 1980: a remarkable golden era and a hard act to follow.

For info, the label 'lightweight' is potentially misleading. There are plenty of tall athletes of imposing physique within the (average) weight limit of 11 stone for men, 9 stone for women. Think of it as more like *normal-weight*. With the open event being more like a *giant-weight* category.

Lightweights, both men and women, had to wait until 1996 for inclusion as an Olympic event category. And now, after a good run of over 20 years, lightweights look set to be phased out entirely soon, despite it being some of the best (closest, fairest, most tactical and skilful) racing of the Games. But this author is biased.

There are reams I could write about the race, and about the gut-busting semi-final of a few days earlier, where GB had just beaten off the French, to secure our place in the final. Of twelve top international crews, we had made the final cut of six. But it wasn't to be our day. A combination of things – some might label excuses, yet painfully real – meant we finished in sixth place. Last.

My memories of that year are embodied. Muscle memory. Vivid. We don't forget events that happen with such lucidity. Business was unfinished. And much of that memory is RED. And business was unfinished...

Why red? Because the lightweight squad was sponsored by MOBIL Oil. Talking of business: a bright red logo, and an all red (carbon-fibre) boat. Even forty years ago, sport was being soaked in (red) greenwash: sportwash.

MOBIL Oil knew – and also knew what they had to do to keep all sports fans off their scent, and off their C-suite backs. And keep their logo on ours: on the backs of our track suits. The corporate leadership team of Mobil should be red faced. And as I mentioned, this story is one of 'unfinished business'. And of improbable comebacks.

A feature of lightweight rowing is the charge to the line, near the finish. It's never over until it's over. Physiologically, there isn't a brute force and sheer size turbo boost button option, as all athletes are equal in physique. So there are more surprises in the last minute of the race. With everything on the line.

I got married in 1984, and retired prematurely, as did many of that crew, after various debacles within the administration of the sport: selectors behaving like children. Where were the adults back then? Much as Greta still asks now. But I wasn't done. I made a couple of comebacks in the 1980s but eventually hung up my oar and took to rowing coaching. And a career in sustainability leadership. Something to prove perhaps. And I won several awards.

It wasn't until 2010, when I started as a local (eco) radio show presenter that I started to experience regular glimpses of a new gold dream that grabbed me viscerally. It was something I knew I had to do.

How would it be, I thought, if legends from the world of sport spoke out, about issues of justice that mattered to them – be it racism, sexism, or climate and ecological (intergenerational) injustice. All they would have to do (yes !) I thought to myself, while the BBC cameras were on them and the tall winners podium, having just won Olympic gold, was to say, e.g. "I am so happy to have won today, but as well as a sponsored athlete I am also a parent too, and I am desperately concerned about climate change". Before the BBC interview cut away...

And the idea was born, of Champions for Earth. (An early working title was 'Eco Olympians'). Everything about this worked, the more I thought about it. It was an idea whose time had come – or back then, was coming fast.

I studied my history, learnt about the Olympic Project for Human Rights of the 1960s (they hadn't taught me that at school) and I found myself frequently playing a clip on the radio show of Nelson Mandela in the year 2000 on "*The power of sport to change the world*". I started inviting many Olympians onto the show and for every annual Xmas special I would have three Olympians on together. Generally I started to listen closely to – and broadcast – the voice of sport in the arena of climate justice.

Never underestimate the power of sport. Nelson Mandela said it best:

Sport has the power to change the world. It has the power to inspire. It has the power to unite people in a way that little else does. It speaks to youth in a language they understand. Sport can create hope, where once there was only despair. Sport is more powerful than governments in breaking down racial barriers. It laughs in the face of all types of discrimination.

Courage calls to courage and we now have a big team of Champions across different sports and with a good broad diversity of attributes and platforms.

"Never doubt that a small group of sports people will change the world. Indeed, it is the only thing that ever will." – as Margaret Meade almost said. And I didn't... doubt.

Cut to 2023, and Champions for Earth (C4E), now led by a small core team of sporting legends like Olympic champion Etienne Stott (canoe gold, London 2012) Katie Rood (Premier League football), Laura Baldwin (Olympic sailing) and previously Melissa Wilson (Team GB rowing), has blazed a trail of action and inspiration, over the last 4 years in particular, gathering, educating, supporting and inspiring a substantial network of sporting legends- ready to speak up. No one is turned away, as everyone can be a champion for earth, and a growing number of elite sports people are finding the courage to make the most important history of this decade. Of all time.

You can follow C4E's progress via the usual social media @champions4earth and our YouTube channel has videos of past talks from athletes including: Ade Adepitan, Kate Strong, Jacqui Lachmann, and the C4E team; from inspirers including: Jojo Mehta, Hugo Tagholm, Rob Hopkins, Mac Macartney; and from scientists including: Sir David King, Aaron Thierry, Peter Kalmus, Charlie Gardner

Within this compilation of Sporting Tales I hope that this one provides a little evidence that crazy dreams can come true, and that *'impossible is just an* opinion' is an old adage that doesn't only exist within the world of sport, but in the wider race against time, the race for all lives, that we are all starting to run.

The homecoming of an Olympian

Etienne Stott

August 31st 2032

Stepping off the bus, we were met by a wave of cheering and applause, and I could feel the pride, the energy, the love, washing through me. Time has gone weird since we won the Olympic silver medal at Athens '32. These last couple of weeks have been a blur. As the captain I had to do a lot of media interviews, but we also had some partying to do. The first one was just with the team and because we knew we'd be on TV live the next morning, we did take it slightly easy (only slightly!). But the Team GB party after the closing ceremony was just epic. We released the tension of these past few weeks, past few months – maybe even the tension of my lifetime...

I didn't quite get what I wanted all those years ago, and it stung a bit, but I know I won't be moaning. I'm proud of what I did, what we did. We represented our values and stood tall when we were asked. The Aussies were just better. I've got no problem with that and besides, it's history now. I worked hard, I gave it everything, but I know I was lucky. So lucky. In so many ways.

When we were out there, we knew we had the support of the country, but what really mattered to us was that we had the support of our town. Literally everyone was pulling for us. Tonnes of people watched our training sessions and shared the campaign with us. They knew us, we knew them. We were connected together. Our club is more than a place to do sport. People come and hang out during the days and evenings, there's always stuff going on, music and shows and stuff. I remember the club president sent a video out to us before our event. He got messages from the kitchen crew who had made a special plant-based dish in our honour. All the kids from the youth teams wished us well too, as well as the facilities team (the gardeners had made a special Olympic display in the wall garden).

A section of the video was taken looking out over the main fan hub in town on the night of the opening ceremony. I swear the whole town was there! After England men won the football World Cup two years ago, there was some sort of magic energy bottled up in there and it was great to see it so full. The atmosphere looked incredible. I felt that love and I knew that no matter how we did at the Games, how I myself performed, they'd welcome us all back. I think that freed me of the fear so I could just let my whole self play.

I have to say too, I knew the team was in good shape before we left, but you're never quite sure. Last year we got bronze in the European Cup and the year before that we were 5th in the Worlds. Since we decided to let go of all the international tour events and have just one focus each year (nowadays, each Olympiad goes: Continentals, Worlds, Continentals, Olympics), we periodised our training with some really deep developmental blocks, getting right back to the foundations. We used to do so many events that it was tough to really develop our technique. But I think a key advantage for us has been how creative we've been with our training methods and also how we've kept our competitive sharpness. We took our individual technique and tactics on a journey of play and exploration. That period was so much fun and just so nourishing. We felt like kids again, learning and just blowing our minds with what we came up with as we bounced off each other! It was a challenge to put this new stuff to the test competitively, but we got very clever around simulating teams and the pressure of events.

One of the coolest things we did in this area was getting ganged up on by the youth team players! I actually loved those sessions where they outnumbered us 5:1. There was one session a few weeks before we left which I'll never forget. I went deep into the zone.

It was like I was in my body, but also flying above the match. I had this intense, but effortless awareness.

I knew where the opposition were, where they were moving, what was opening up. It was crazy. I somehow just knew where my teammates were going to be before I made my moves. For about 20 minutes in that match it was like bullet time in the Matrix (you know the old-school original version with Keanu Reeves, from back in the day). To be honest, I could have retired there and then. It was my pinnacle performance and a shade or two better than what I brought at the Games. And I think it gave the town a glimpse of what we might be capable of at the Olympics. Those practice events, beamed to fan hubs across the country, but with half the town watching in person, really helped build the hype around the team, but it also gave us confidence that we had the skills to handle performing in the spotlight.

I can't not talk about the decision to relocate the Games to Athens. It made sense, but that was a big call for the International Olympic Committee and the Brisbane organising team. That was tough. It was toughest for the Aussies, I can imagine it. But they know better than some how destabilised the climate has got in these last few years and I think it was brave of them to admit that it made better sense to have the Olympics in one place from now on. They had the fires, but since they lost the coral reef, it's got real for them. Yeah, they had to fly for some of their journey to Athens, and so did a few other teams, but the overall carbon reduction was important and it was good to show it could be done. It seemed like they adapted really well to the travelling, fair credit to them.

I remember after LA thinking to myself that getting to Brisbane for the next one, my carbon emissions would be difficult on my conscience. I want to minimise my impact on the planet, just like everyone else. So yeah, call it a fairytale, but I think it worked out nice enough for the Aussies to get the gold. They lost something, but they gained too. And man, did they step up! Their prep and analysis must have been very smart. They knew their stuff and had clearly worked on the style they needed to beat us, despite being on the other side of the world!

Fair play to the Greeks too though. They hosted us well, rewilding and upgrading their venues from 2004. It was a beautiful blend of old, new, natural and man-made. The commitment shown to bringing the athletes in from around the world in the lowest carbon way possible was impressive and I really liked the way Games organisers made the trip worthwhile. There were World Cup events in the venue before, which gave a chance to test the consistency of the athletes (which I think think reveals true champion class, as well as the one-off moments of glory) and the way they worked it out so the European teams didn't get into the venue more than the other countries actually levelled the playing field in favour of the countries that can't get their teams around so easily. Saving the Olympic arena for the Olympics is a tricky shout, but it makes sense. By the time the next one comes about, the data links and the immersive crowd experience stuff will be absolutely perfect, I expect, and I am looking forward to watching that one at the fan hub in town! People don't know yet, but this was my last year doing sport at this level.

Getting into the club tonight was special. It was like my senses were switched on to max! I have been away for two months all-told, and the season is turning. The air seemed fresher than before. I think there must have been some rain whilst I was away. We'd been struggling with that before we left. I could smell the flowers in the meadows and there were some good aromas wafting out of people's houses. We went past a couple of suburb hubs on our way and they were getting ready to watch our homecoming live on the local broadcast. They'd put a special flag on the bus and people were cheering us from the pavements and balconies, waving flags and honking horns. Kids were pedalling alongside and there was a giant peloton of scooters. It was wild!

As we walked through the doors into the main hall of the community sport hub, the roof nearly lifted off with the cheer! I spotted a few of the other local heroes down at the front and there were a tonne of old folk sat there near them. And then the families were there on the stage. I could see my lot beaming from where I was! That was something. My little sister has been getting into her road cycling more. She's only young, but you can see her confidence growing. She's not the

best in her year, it might be that she doesn't get to an elite level, but you just can't tell. The thing that makes me happy is that nowadays kids are learning about winning and losing in sport, so it's not quite as black and white as when I started out. And although I am a specialist, most kids now just do a fair bit of all sorts.

I don't quite know how, but they just play around in different sports and I've noticed that people are combining sports to make new hybrids in ways that must be a lot of fun. My elder brother is stoked on sport, but he's not competitive. I think he just likes the vibe of the running club because his mates are there. As for my folks, well, what can I say? – they're my folks! They are both super happy and they know I appreciate what they did for me. My dad taught me that the way you do things is as important as what you actually do and even though he isn't sporty I think this attitude has really come into its own nowadays. And I reckon it was my mum who gave me my sporting brain and body, but the best thing she did was to help me recover when I wasn't doing as well as I wanted.

Well, as I sort of expected, the homecoming celebration went by in a blur. The speech I made went down well. I can't remember what I said, I kinda winged it... I just told the story about our journey to Athens, on the train with the entire Olympic team on it. That was one of the best bits of the whole thing to be fair. We got to know each other more and it felt good to rub shoulders with a few of my heroes! I told them about my event, what it felt like to have been so connected to them even though I was far away.

I think people are worried about what the future may hold, but sport has given everyone a big lift. I'm looking forward to doing a bit more coaching with the really little kids and I also fancy working in the analysis of the international sport database. Even though we won't face the Aussies again til the 2034 Worlds at the earliest (if we both qualify from our continents), I'm going to make sure we've done our homework and I think that the experience of these Games should make us favourites to bring home the European Cup next year. But for the next few weeks, I'm just going to have a rest and hang out with my town.

Poems

Fell run

Clouds gather in elegy
dark shrouds on a hill crest
heads bowed, beneath we thread
patchwork fields, numb running tailors
rocks and hidden drops daring
'go faster', bracken grown
treacherous over track, wobble
as others elbow through
peril every step stops thought
of greater danger, of those succumbed
in pandemic number
 his path made by moving on
reminds we were born to run
how easy it would be
not chasing Ariadne's red flags
to lose the way, forget why
we play with horizons, how
running, we become the landscape
die a little, find life

Andrew Simms

Running

A small child totters onto the playing field
Agog at the space, this massive place
He starts to run, jerky little steps
Tipping terrifyingly this way and that
He can barely walk, but he can run
And so he does – away from the adults
Their arms waving, clutching at him
Spreading their fear like a net
The boy speeds across the grass
Suddenly in gear, all fluid grace
He is running, running, running.

Nicky Saunter

Climate heroes

Last class at college
Pull on your Nikes,
Bike to meet your mates at the park.
No need to logo your belonging.
High fives, fist bumps,
Enough to smile, eyes acknowledge.
It's not Musk or Gates, Davos chumps,
With their shiny silicon dreams
(Send them to the moon, techno clowns)
It's grass roots where leaders are.
This is muddy browns of Hackney Downs
Or ball-bashing cage,
Five-a-side kick about,
Hoody goals.

Grass shoots breaking through paving slabs
Splitting tarmac, cracking concrete,
Ivy and brambles sidling up the wire walls.
Half-time snack, share Gran's cakes,
Grab blackberries from the fence.
Gulp down water,
All you hear is your own gulping
The banter's miles away.
All you feel is the water
Soaking your throat.
And aching limbs with a moment to recover.
Elemental.
This moment is for ever.
This is now.
After the game
Practise the shot again and again.
Not for cash but for the now.
To get better and better,
To get it right, to perfect it,
Mastery over the ball.
That's the reward.
Pints and banter.
Pick Sunday's team.
A day well-played, toiled and won.

James Atkins

166

Running

Running up the mountain
Running down the clock
Running waters flowing fast
Running adrift, aground, amok
In the running for a medal
but running out of breath
For ten days running now
Been running up a debt
Running on reserves of hope
Spirits are running high
Running into friends like you
I'll keep running til I die

Nick Robins

Poetry in emojithon
Is my contribution
To your running rhyming
Passthetiming

Anita Roy

Islands of hope

Jenny Amann

When talking about people driving change, we tend to look at 'others' doing it, admire them for their hard work and get easily caught up in the daily hustle of creating a more sustainable society. What gets pushed into the background is that each one of us is part of one or more networks trying to do the best we can to limit global warming and accelerate rapid transitions in sport and beyond. We try to get athletes on board, fans engaged, and to get clubs, leagues and associations to act on climate change, drive change amongst their peers and use their power to demand change from the industry and politics.

Yet who is 'we'? – A mix of dedicated and driven practitioners, researchers, activists committed to do something about climate change and its consequences, which affect us all – with the ones contributing the least to the crisis being affected by it the most.

Even though 'sustainability' seems to have made it into the mainstream, making sure actors in sport (and beyond) apply a holistic understanding of the concept rather than just trying to tick a box and focus on the commercial side of it alone, requires lots of staying power, consideration, and tactfulness from those of us pushing for deeper societal transformations. Such transformations are necessary, given that our aim is to reduce greenhouse gas emissions in order to keep global warming below 1.5°C as "mindsets, norms, rules, institutions, and policies that support unsustainable resource use and practices"[13] are the underlying drivers of climate change.

Whilst being able to work on something that we are all very passionate about – sustainability and sports – being the ones pushing for the big changes frequently comes at the expense of our own needs and/or feels like taking one step forward and two steps back, which can feel exhausting.

This begs the question of *who or what pushes and refuels us*?

For me, being able to surround myself regularly with like-minded people who are equally trying to make the seemingly impossible possible gives me hope and energises me. Therefore, this piece is about emphasising the importance of networks – not just the ones that form to drive social change, but particularly the ones that allow us to sit back, reflect, and take a breath while we share and discuss the newest

---

13   (Leichenko and O'Brien 2019, 43)

developments and insights, plan collaborations, offer and receive advice and vent. For me, such networks are my islands of hope in a warming world. Tackling climate change requires collective action or, drawing on sporting terminology, a team effort. All the more important to recognize and dedicate more time to those islands and people that give us hope and help us recharge on this hectic and ambitious mission to sustain sports and protect the planet we play them on.

Astro/Life

Judith Dean

I used to play a lot of hockey. In 1982, after playing on turf for 4 years, clods and all, I was invited with some other Essex teenagers to attend a residential coaching weekend at Crystal Palace to play on their new Astroturf pitch. I'd previously played on a high quality turf pitch, as well as (mostly) much poorer ones.

My first encounter with Astroturf was amazing – the ball could be propelled much faster, more smoothly, more easily, more predictably, without bouncing up from the inevitable undulations experienced on an earth pitch, so often exacerbated by poor or even careless play. Running around on Astroturf in trainers rather than boots I felt lighter and freer, stronger; and there was no mud to clean off afterwards.

At that time in the UK Astroturf was still very new. I stopped playing hockey a couple of years later, before it had been introduced more widely, so didn't play on it again until I decided to have another go at the game in the mid-90s, by which time all the pitches I subsequently played on were Astroturf. Whilst wonderful to be outside, running around, reading the game, etc, it was also much duller: the reading and caring for the ground previously integral to the game was gone. As was the smell of the earth and its varying states – from soft, muddy, slippery to rock hard. I played on Astroturf for a couple of years before giving up.

Some years later on Hampstead Heath I stumbled across an informal 'turn up if you can' open-to-all weekly game that was played at that time on something of a slope: an unmaintained, decidedly rough, bumpy, grassy clearing – easily the worst 'pitch' I'd ever played on.

Playing regularly until too much, I'd get there early because of my rather long bike ride, and so witness the other players arrive through the trees and out of the bushes, from Autumn, through Winter and into Spring, to hit a ball around with each other in the midst of that forever changing, breathing, living, pulsating, vibrant environment, more than a tonic for the soul: our lifeblood.

These days I practice qigong.

Porth Ergh

Francesca Willow

When I crouched I placed my hands on the ground to feel for the cold that once lingered there. Beneath the gravel, clustered between my fingers and cutting into my palms, I knew the memory remained. The earth was dark and compacted; blue-black and still soft underfoot. The 31st day was here, and it was coming to an end.

We marked the wassail, though dates continued to shift and patterns remained unpredictable. For now, we timed it with the arrival of the 31st, before the scorching heat and the incessant rain began. The moment of inhalation before the year was unleashed. We poured cider, saved from the months before, on the roots of the trees. We took bread, soaked in the same bowl, and hung it from their branches to sustain them through the difficult days to come. Children manouevred their balls through the gaps between the trunks, crooked goalposts with nets only they could see. We danced through the orchard, no particular steps necessary, banging the metal we brought from home. Sticks to hit the pots and mugs in our hands, branches to weave into rudimentary circles for our heads. Carefully preserved leaves, still delicate, fresh and green, blurred our vision and fell between our steps, gently drifting through their descent. From the corners of our eyes, it almost looked like the weather we'd once heard of.

Despite it all, we still felt the joy.

We sung and stamped, calling the trees to wake up once more. Jumped in whirls that replaced the glistening white eddies we hadn't seen in a long, long time. We ran races and jumped hurdles, brought out the small balls we'd fashioned and formed makeshift teams to share the bats whittled from old branches the year before, families shouting from the sidelines. Our voices rose far beyond the bare, twisted branches that clawed the sky; words drifting out on waves that had grown ever-harsher, but someone, somewhere, still caught the echoes. The trees had adapted, fruit came in erratic bursts and their slumber was more of a prolonged nap. But they gave generously when they could, and so we still came to rouse them. And we felt the gratitude in our bones, where the chill no longer reached. It was a happiness we had adapted, carved from the flesh of our memories and the realities of the present, and it was still ours to hold to.

The day ended early. Children were taken to their beds as the adult preparations for day 'one' began. The end of the winter month meant a changing of the windows, the bedspreads, the doorways. The clearing out of storm drains and ditches. The securing of polytunnels and covering of vulnerable soils. Anything to keep the air from stagnating and the water from collecting where it shouldn't. Anything to protect the harvests we relied on.

I was cleaning the last of the bowls when I heard it, half growl half shout, and I knew that I should be afraid. It was like nothing in my memory: inhuman and impossibly loud, a rumbling thunder rolling in from the water. No one else was close and the village nearby remained undisturbed, so absorbed in preparation that no one else seemed to hear. Resolve rooted inside me, calling me to follow before I could start to doubt.

The orchard sloped down towards the sea, slowly morphing into white sand and granite, black rocks jutting through the breakers at low tide. Among them, a creature, also lying low in the waters of the bay. I caught a glimpse of an eye, impossibly large and shining above the foaming waves, scales glistening incandescent, refracting sunlight into bright flecks of rainbow. A flash of white. A smile, or something like it, impossible to fully tell. Empty of the fear that should've sprung between my ribs, I began to run. Sand kicked up at my heels, the beach stretching long and low as I reached the edge. I rested my palm to the surface, each year warmer than the last, and felt a shiver of anticipation. The water trembled with a low hum, the giant speaking once more, and in an instant I recognised her.

Or perhaps, the idea of her. A tale from centuries ago, when breezes could blow through and the sea could sting with cold. Places where it could be dry for days; others where water would freeze long enough to skate on or glide down. A different world, where she twisted her way through children's tales, always leading them to treasure, but never quite made a clear photograph. And yet here she was.

'Hello, Morgawr!' I shouted above the noise of the rolling sea. 'Thank you for revealing yourself to me!'

I bowed, tilting at the waist, trying to imbue the reverence of the heroes from my childhood stories. She had offered herself up to me, and I didn't want to disrespect this small miracle. There was no reply beyond a rumbling, but she fixed me with a steady gaze. Her eyes glinted black as she inclined her head and slowly turned away, shimmering colour arcing in her wake. And so I followed.

She never went too fast, but she stayed just out of reach. Even when beaches turned to rocky cliffs and I had to wade, then swim, to continue. The waves stilled around her, and the water was pleasantly warm, a classic February day before it became unbearably hot in a month or two. My sodden clothes dragged me down, but I didn't grow tired. Time seemed to blur into both a moment and a marathon, and I kept following for as long as she kept moving. The horizon stretched beyond us like we were the only two beings on the earth. And I felt how impossibly small I was. But I knew I wasn't alone, and when she finally stopped she turned her face to me once more, urging me towards a large cove before us. I didn't recognise this part of the coastline; cliffs jutting wildly to block it from view from above. If you didn't come by sea, you'd never know it was here. With fishing abandoned decades ago, when had someone last passed by this place?

The ground looked so white it glittered, and as I pushed myself from the balmy waves and stepped across the stones I felt something I'd never known before. My feet were stinging.

'Excuse me, Morgawr!' I shouted back towards to sea, 'do you know the meaning of this?'

She seemed to smile once more, urging me forward with her silence. I stepped through the white sand towards rolling dunes, but it didn't feel as it normally did. I tried to think like the scientists in the village, observing what was different. The... the wetness wasn't quite right, was that it? Something about it was painful to me but I couldn't find the words. My bare feet were slowly changing colour, redness creeping up my toes as they turned stiff. That definitely wasn't normal.

A dune towered before me, something blue glinting at its peak. I climbed up, my feet making deep indentations in the strange sand, and found it to be a plastic vessel, a small rope attached to one side. In the middle, an indentation for sitting, so I continued my path of observation by placing myself inside. It was sturdy, slightly curved, the rope long enough to be held in my hands as if to steer in some rudimentary fashion. I shuffled back and forth, lightly pulling the rope to see if this revealed the vessel's secrets. I grew more animated in my exploration, enjoying this newfound discovery until, without realising, I tipped the entire thing off balance.

Before I could stop myself, we began to slide down the dune. Steep and long, we picked up speed rapidly. The air whipped my face as I screamed, terror and joy making fascinating swirls in my chest. Shouts of fear turned to delight and surprise, rippling through the air to drown out the sea, the impossible whiteness zoomed all around me and filled up everything in my eyesight. It was all white and it was all fast and it was all wonder. I pulled the rope once more, swinging from left to right in sweeping curves, winding my way towards the earth and yet hovering above it. I was alive and I was flying.

And then it was over, the vessel tipped and I rolled out into the whiteness, my whole self sinking into it and leaving an imprint of my body in the snow. I lay on my back and swung my arms up and down around me, giving myself wings.

'I know what this is, Morgawr!' I screamed to the sky. 'This is snow!'

I threw handfuls in the air, my fingers screaming as they felt cold for the very first time. My blood was rushing to the centre of myself, keeping my organs safe as my hands and feet became stiffer and stiffer. It was the best pain I'd ever felt.

When I finally sat up, tired of rolling around in delight alone, I saw she was already on her way once again. A dark shadow retreating into the sun. There were tears in my eyes as I waved goodbye.

When I crouched I placed my hands on the ground to feel the cold on my palms again. When I brought the adults here, insisting that pulling the boats from storage would be more than worth their while, it hadn't taken long for the word to spread through the village.

'Some kind of micro-climate is our working theory' one of the scientists told me. 'If we can figure out the conditions that led to this, who knows what breakthroughs could follow... But how on earth did you know this was all the way out here?'

I smiled as I retreated, dragging myself up the rolling dunes with a crowd of eager children in my wake.

'It's a long story, remind me to tell you when we've finished sledging!"

Contributors

Jenny Amann is a Doctoral Researcher at the Loughborough University, a member of the Sport Ecology Group's Graduate Mentorship Programme and a Werder Bremen fan. Her main research focus is on using football as an alternative way to communicate climate change and inspire collective climate action. Beyond that, she is looking into the potential of football fans to drive societal change more broadly.

James Atkins is an entrepreneur and football fan who founded Planet Super League, a company that is using football and gamification to inspire fans to take climate actions, repeat them and share them.

Laura Baldwin represented Team GB at the Athens 2004 Olympic Games in the sport of sailing. At her peak she was World Ranked #2. Sharing her passion and knowledge through coaching at the London 2012 Olympics with the Australian Team and Rio 2016 with the Hungarian Team. Since 2019 Laura, now a mother, has been focused on environmental protection through frontline activism, as a spokesperson for Extinction Rebellion UK, with community action through her local Transition Town, leading on planting trees and establishing community food gardens etc, through politics both nationally and internationally having served for three years on the Green Party of England and Wales Executive and Global Greens Climate Emergency Working Group strategising for COP conferences. Laura is one of four leading Champions For Earth that aims to educate, inspire and support past and present sports people to speak and act for climate and nature.

Freddie Daley is a campaigner for Badvertising, leading their work on sport and sponsorship. He facilitates the Cool Down Sport For Climate Action Network and is an academic at the University of Sussex working on energy transitions and phasing out fossil fuels.

Judith Dean is a practicing artist and a Senior Lecturer in Fine Arts at the University of the West of England. Selected solo exhibitions include One Thing and the Others, Bodenrader, Chicago, 2024, bodenrader.com/judith-dean, and New Builds / Bilds (The Image in Perspective), South Parade, London, 2023, southparade.biz/judith-dean. She lives and works in London, made a trophy from recycled sports equipment for the World COP26 (a 'play fair' football competition at the 2021 Glasgow, COP26 climate conference), and used to throw the javelin.

David Goldblatt lives in Bristol, the Bermuda Triangle of football success. In 2015 he won the William Hill Sports Book of the Year Award for The Game of Our Lives:The Meaning and Making of English Football and the Sports Story of the Year at the Foreign Press Association Media Awards for his article for The Guardian Long Read, The prison where murderers play for Manchester United. He is also an academic, and has lectured on the sociology of sport at Bristol University and Pitzer College, and is author of The Games: A Global History of the Olympics, published in 2016 by Macmillan in the UK and WW Norton in the US.

Damian Hall is a runner, coach, author and activist. He is a record-breaking ultramarathon runner who represented Great Britain aged 40 and continues to record competitive results in the world's toughest races (mostly powered by tea). He is also a recovering journalist with 20-plus years' experience of writing for, sub-editing on and editing newspapers, magazines, websites and books, specialising in sport, travel and the great outdoors. He is author of several books, including the bestselling In It For The Long Run and award-nominated We Can't Run Away From This. Damian is also co-founder of The Green Runners, a regular at climate protests, has boycotted races with high-carbon sponsors and is an outspoken critic of sportswashing. Damian has pledged to fly once a year maximum for running, has turned Full Annoying Vegan and exhibits an appropriately dodgy haircut.

Dave Hampton has been a passionate sustainability professional for more than 30 years. In his younger days, he rowed for Great Britain. Having studied engineering at Cambridge University, during the 1990's Dave led the team that created the world's first method for measuring the environmental performance of buildings and infrastructure (BREEAM) – now used in 80 countries worldwide. Since 2005, as the Carbon Coach, he has advised and inspired celebrities and organisations to improve their sustainability footprints. Champions for Earth (launched in 2018) has been a dream of his since the London Olympics. Dave has hosted The Eco Show weekly on Marlow FM since 2010. He is a Director of the Association of Sustainability Practitioners and a judge on the Global Good Awards. He has been a climate activist since 2005.

Joe Hodge graduated from the School of Veterinary Medicine and Science at the University of Nottingham in 2012 and practiced as a veterinary surgeon for six years. He then transitioned to a career as a creative and medical writer, supporting charities through a writing collective called RubyDuke. Sport has always been a significant part of Joe's life, from handcrafting cricket bats in his spare time to playing golf, tennis, and cricket recreationally. Through his charity work, he hopes to promote a more accessible and sustainable future for sport for everyone.

Anna Jonsson is a co-founder of New Weather Sweden. With more than twenty years in environmental policy and in the environmental movement, she has worked extensively with various environmental issues and in several roles. She also has broad experience of leading conversations and creative processes as a screenwriter, workshop leader and moderator. Anna has her roots in the environmental movement and has been chairman of the Swedish Field Biologists and Friends of the Earth Sweden. In those roles, she worked to strengthen the voice of the environmental movement through political influence. From 2007, she worked at the Green Party in the Swedish Parliament with a focus on issues such as traffic and the environment, as well as as head of the environment and foreign team. From 2018 until early 2021 Anna has worked at the Ministry of the Environment as a political expert and at the Prime Minister's Committee on the Environment, Climate and Biodiversity. Anna has previously been an expert in the Environmental Objectives Council and the Environmental Protection Agency. The work in environmental policy alternates Anna with assignments in theater and music with the environmental cabaret group Sweet Dreams.

Geoff Mead is a storyteller, consultant, and the author of two books on the power of stories and storytelling: Coming Home to Story: Storytelling Beyond Happily Ever After (Vala, 2011) and Telling the Story: The Heart and Soul of Successful Leadership (Jossey-Bass, 2014). He is the founder of Narrative Leadership Associates, a consultancy focused on the use of storytelling for sustainable leadership. As an organizational consultant, keynote speaker and workshop leader, he has taken his work on narrative leadership onto the shopfloors and into the boardrooms of blue chip companies, charities, universities and government departments, for the past two decades (www.narrativeleadership.com). Geoff performs traditional stories at International Festivals and storytelling clubs and runs story-based workshops in the UK and as far afield as Spain, Canada and Japan.

Deborah Rim Moiso lives in Central Italy, taking care of a smallholding and working as a facilitator of participatory processes. She has published short stories in Italian and English, including in the previous Knock Twice, Knock Three Times, and Contagious Tales collections, and a non-fiction book on facilitation, in Italian (Facilitiamoci!). This story is inspired by her involvement as participatory process specialist working in a project to support coexistence of local (human) communities and Marsican bears. Deborah hopes to contribute to rewilding the Apennines, as well as your imagination.

Benjamin Mole is a Doctoral Researcher at Loughborough University (London) focused on sport and sustainability. Based largely on the planetary boundaries literature, Benjamin is concerned for the planet's future, particularly in the context of justice for marginalised regions, groups and biodiversity. Ben is from South Africa and his work endeavours to establish better representation for southern Africa, both as a source of knowledge and as an area to be protected from the potential mistakes of more 'developed' regions. Despite being a sports fanatic, Benjamin acknowledges the impact elite sport has on the world and seeks fair and practical alternative structures. In this vein, his work focuses on community structures around sport.

Chris Nichols lives on Dartmoor. He's a long distance walker. Having walked the 1,000 km of the South West Coast Path, he next set out to walk the borders and coasts of Wales. When he's not walking or getting to know his baby grand-daughter, he is co-founder of the collaborative hub <u>Gameshift.co.uk.</u>

Verity Ockenden is a professional runner for On Running. She has been competing for Great Britain on the track and the mud since 2018, and won a European Bronze medal over 3000m at the Indoor Championships in Toruń, 2021. A literature graduate with a passion for poetry, Verity now lives and trains in Italy where she writes for Athletics Weekly amongst other publications.

Mark Perryman is the co-founder of the self-styled 'sporting outfitters of intellectual distinction'; aka Philosophy Football and has written widely on sport including Why The Olympics Aren't Good For Us and How They Can Be.

Matt Rendell has written on sport for the BBC, ITV and Channel 4, including presenting British coverage of the Tour de France. His book Kings of the Mountains: How Colombia's Cycling Heroes Changed their Nation's History (Aurum Press 2002) was described in The Times as 'meticulous, elegant and sensitive.' His Channel 4 documentary about sport in Colombia and Ecuador, also called Kings of the Mountains, was described in The Observer as 'a gem, telling us more about the essence of sport in under an hour than a season's worth of Premiership matches.'

Nick Robins is a sustainable investor and historian who works as Professor in Practice at the London School of Economics. He is author of The Corporation that Changed the World: How the East India Company Shaped the Modern Multinational (2012).

Anita Roy is a writer, editor and cloud-maker. Her books include Gifts of Gravity and Light, A Year in Kingcombe and Gravepyres School for the Recently Deceased. She is a regular contributor to the Guardian's Country Diary column.

Nicky Saunter is a serial collaborator and starter of sustainable things, including the Boston Tea Party coffee house group, The Woolly Shepherd acoustics firm, natural training social enterprise Learning from the Land and most recently the wildlife and landscape restoration charity, Beaver Trust. In between, she writes poems and stories, makes animal masks to wear at protests and prints monochrome photographs, heavily influenced by her rural life. If she could change into an animal, she would.

Andrew Simms is an author, political economist and campaigner. He co-authored the original Green New Deal, came up with Earth Overshoot Day, and jointly proposed the Fossil Fuel Non Proliferation Treaty (with Prof Peter Newell). He is co-director of the New Weather Institute, coordinator of the Rapid Transition Alliance, assistant director of Scientists for Global Responsibility, and a research associate at the University of Sussex. He set up and coordinates the Badvertising campaign to stop adverts fuelling the climate emergency and his books include Cancel the Apocalypse, Ecological Debt, the heterodox guide, Economics: A Crash Course, and Badvertising. When not campaigning, Andrew dips his feet into running with his local community athletics club, and his mind into words and poetry.

Caroline Staudt is an attorney turned sustainability advocate. She focuses her work on helping individuals, organizations, and municipalities increase their climate shadows (not to be confused with their carbon footprints) through advising and educating around the impact of overconsumption of things and resources, speaking out for systemic and policy changes, and promoting positive civic behavior. In her spare time, Caroline runs marathons and ultra marathons and volunteers her time with The Green Runners, a group intent on "running without the footprint." Her blog, The Green Ostrich, provides education around the environmental impact of running, the clothing industry, and the intersection of the two. She lives in

Boston, Massachusetts, USA with her husband, two children, and dog.

Etienne Stott won the Gold Medal at the London 2012 Olympics in the sport of canoe slalom, with his crew-mate Tim Baillie and is now an environmental activist and campaigner. After retiring from elite sport in 2016, Etienne finished an Open University degree in psychology to add to the practical knowledge gained through his athletic career. With a foundation of belief in human potential and the energy of an elite athlete, Etienne now uses his Olympic platform to inspire action on the environmental crisis. He is a co-founder of the Champions for Earth campaign group, which harnesses the power of sport to tackle the planetary emergency. Etienne is also an outspoken member of Extinction Rebellion, and has taken part in many peaceful direct action protests.

Francesca Willow is an artist, writer and climate justice activist based in Cornwall. Her work aims to take a holistic approach to climate justice, culture, and regenerative futures, while her activism focuses on campaigning against the fossil fuel industry's involvement in arts and culture. You can find Francesca's work @ethicalunicorn everywhere on the internet, or follow her campaigning with Badvertising, Clean Creatives, BP or not BP? and the Stop Rosebank campaign.

the **sport** for
climate action
network

cooldownclimate.org

Cool Down is a network that believes sport and the climate emergency are inseparable. Its members campaign to raise awareness, challenge those polluting sport, and help lead the way on rapid transition. It was initiated by the New Weather Institute and the Rapid Transition Alliance.

Athletes of the World	athletesoftheworld.org
Active Humber	activehumber.co.uk
British Association for Sustainability in Sport (BASIS)	basis.org.uk
Champions for Earth	championsforearth.com
Common Goal	common-goal.org
Football Supporters Europe	fanseurope.org

Football Ecologie (France)	football-ecology.org/fr
Football For Future	footballforfuture.org
Football Supporters Association (England)	thefsa.org.uk
Frontrunners (Australia)	frontrunners.org.au
Fossil Free Football	fossilfreefootball.org
Philosophy Football	philosophyfootball.com
Planet Earth Games	planetearthgames.org
Pledgeball	pledgeball.org
Save Our Snow (Sweden) saveoursnow	badvertising.se/
Spirit of Football (International)	spiritoffootball.com
Spirit of Football Germany	spirit-of-football.de
Sport LOCAL for life	sport-local.earth
Street Football World	See: common-goal.org
Supporters Direct Europe	sdeurope.eu
Supporters Direct Scotland	supporters-direct.scot
The Green Runners (UK)	thegreenrunners.com
Youth Sport Uganda (Uganda)	youthsportuganda.org

THE REAL
PRESS

New Weather
Institute

Rapid Transition
Alliance

therealpress.co.uk

newweather.org

rapidtransition.org